Black President Collection
Season 3, Episodes 1-2
The Conclusion

Black President Collection
Season 3, Episodes 1-2
The Conclusion

Brenda Hampton Entertainment

Brenda Hampton Entertainment
P.O. Box 773
Bridgeton, MO 63044

Black President Collection: Season 3

Printed in the United States of America

This is a work of fiction. Any references or similarities to actual events, real people, living or dead, or to real locales are intended to give the novel a sense of reality. Any similarity in other names, characters, places, and incidents is entirely coincidental.

ISBN 13: 978-1986821186
ISBN 10: 1986821188

Black President: Drama in the White House
Season 3, Episode 1

President of the United States, Stephen C. Jefferson

For the past several weeks, I had been numb. Michelle's death had taken a toll on me. It was difficult for me to get back into the swing of things at the White House. I definitely hadn't been myself, and I kept saying I would do better. No more killings, no more scandals . . . nothing. It was unfortunate that I kept losing people I cared about the most. I couldn't help but to think all of this revolved around karma. It had to be payback—there was no other way to look at it. So with that in mind, I vowed to start over, ignore my enemies and focus more on what I came here to do. That was to serve the American people.

For the most part, I had been quiet as a mouse. If it hadn't been for my chief of staff, Andrew, things wouldn't have gotten done. I had to give credit to Vice President Bass who had stepped up too. She didn't know the specifics of my relationship with Michelle, nor did she know how much losing her had affected me. No one knew, mainly because I had mastered keeping things bottled up inside. The truth was, this was a hurt I hadn't felt before. A tremendous blow to me, simply because I'd had high hopes for us. I hadn't experienced happiness like I'd done with Michelle in a long time. And at the snap of my fingers that happiness had dissipated, thanks to my mother. My lousy ass mother who couldn't get her drinking under control. I blamed her for everything. There was nothing she could say or do to make me forgive her for this. Not this time, no. She needed to pay for what she'd done, and I wanted her in jail for the rest of her life.

As for the first lady, Raynetta, she'd been missing in action. I spotted her a few times at the White House; it was obvious she was trying to avoid me. Not because of what had happened to Michelle, but because she had been on tour promoting that damn book. I was pissed about it, especially since she'd made it all about me. It didn't surprise me so many Americans were interested in reading about the garbage she had put in there. Some of it was true, some not. Nonetheless, it didn't stop the media from talking about it and many media outlets were trying to obtain an interview with me to discuss it. My strategy, for now, was to stay silent. Raynetta was already out there talking about it, and as I sat on the sofa in the Oval Office, still in my pajama pants and T-shirt, I tuned in to the Morning Show.

"I read through the entire first installment in less than a few hours," the newscaster bragged to Raynetta who sat on a circular sofa across from her. "I'm totally in awe and the book was a tease. Please tell me there's more to come."

Raynetta crossed her long legs, sat with good posture and presented some class. She swooped part of her curled hair behind her ears, making sure everyone could see the smile on her face and glee in her eyes.

"I can promise you there will be more," she admitted. "My publisher decided to make Black President an ongoing series. What you've read is only the tip of the iceberg."

While holding the book in her hand, the newscaster flipped through several pages. She blushed, cleared her throat and grinned as she read an excerpt.

"No questions about it, the president was in command. He lifted my legs, kissing them tenderly before placing them over his broad shoulders. The pace increased and rhythm changed, right after he journeyed a little bit deeper. It hurt, but in a good way. Mr. President was a fantastic lover. I'd never met a man to smack it up, flip it, taste it and rub it all down at the same time, like he'd done. My juices boiled over and sweat rained on our naked bodies that made sweet music for almost the entire night. I wasn't sure *how we were going to keep this a secret, but we would soon find out that cameras, even on Air Force One, revealed everything."*

The newscaster sighed while examining Raynetta's impassive demeanor. *"This reads like an erotic romance novel, and those words were allegedly spoken from a reporter, Chanel Hamilton, who used to work for this network. If you weren't on Air Force One that day, how do you know what her thoughts were in the moment? Have you spoken to Chanel and did she give you permission to share her experience? Or did the president relay her words to you? More than anything, how does all of this make you feel? Surely, you're troubled by the president's, well, his actions."*

Raynetta continued to smile as if she wasn't the least bit bothered.

"I've had plenty of conversations with Chanel Hamilton. She was always willing to share every detail of her time with my husband. My feelings never mattered much to anyone, but today I'm feeling pretty darn good. Black President was difficult for me to write, and as the story continues, everyone will get a good idea about many of the challenges some first ladies face. It's not easy being married to a president, but no matter what, many of us continue to stand by our husbands."

"Well, that's something I will never understand. After reading the first installment, I'm shocked you're still at the White House. I can only imagine what the following books will reveal, so I have to ask you again. Are you still committed to your marriage? Without going into details, there seems to be a lot going on with the president. We don't know what's true and what's not, but to ignore everything we've heard and read would be foolish."

Like always, Raynetta had an answer for everything. She was prepared and she knew exactly what to say to keep the American people on her side.

"I will remain committed to the president because of my promise to God. Nothing that the president does surprises me, and the good thing is he loves this country. He is in the process of

making some historic changes. And when all is said and done neither of us will be leaving the White House. Pertaining to what's true or not in my book, that'll be up to the American people to decide. I'm just expressing how I feel, and this book was a great opportunity for me to let everyone get a peek at some of the things that transpire inside of the White House."

"You gave us more than just a peek. We want to know more. Chanel Hamilton is here today to share her side of the story and clear up any misunderstandings about her brief encounters with the president. I hope you don't mind if we invited her here today."

Raynetta slightly rolled her eyes and shrugged her shoulders. She appeared caught off guard.

"As a very bold woman, Chanel has a right to speak up and say what she wishes about her time with a married man. This should be interesting, so please invite her to come out and join us."

The newscaster stood to introduce Chanel. As she entered the set, I reached for the remote to turn off the TV. I predicted the Morning Show was about to get real messy. That was right up Raynetta's alley; I was sure she would have a good time while in the presence of a woman I still considered one of my many enemies. Well, in my opinion, both of them were.

I stood and stretched. My pajama pants were wrinkled and my T-shirt had holes in it. My hair needed to be washed—waves were barely there. I had even grown a rugged beard which needed a trim. And even though morning exercise always made me feel better, I hadn't done one sit-up. I didn't know who or what would get me out of the slump I was in. Not even Andrew's news about Mr. McNeil's body being found moved me. Andrew came into the Oval Office to tell me about it. Little did he know, his news was old news to me. Alex, a secret agent on my personal payroll, had handled his business with that issue and done it well.

"This is tragic," Andrew said while holding several papers and a binder in his hand. His glasses were at the tip of his nose as he peered over them to observe my reaction. "I never liked the man, but the person who robbed and killed him should be arrested. The FBI is investigating. As soon as I find out more I will let you know."

All I did was nod. My muscles felt tight, so I lifted my arms above my head, pulled and stretched again.

"Great," I said disinterested. "What else?"

"Our staff meeting is still at noon, you have to honor the three soldiers we discussed in the East Room at four and you must be in attendance at a fundraiser tonight. Senator Wilson is counting on you to be there and speak on his behalf. I know you don't feel up to it, Mr. President, but you have to start being your old self again. Even though you were a pain in the ass, I kind of miss hearing you yell at people."

I ignored Andrew and walked over to the Resolute desk. After I fell back in the chair, I yawned and scratched my head.

"Let Senator Wilson know I won't be attending the fundraiser tonight. He can get someone else to speak on his behalf. After I shower and change clothes, I'll see you at the staff meeting. Tell Sam to cancel the press briefing today so he can attend the ceremony in the East Room with us. I don't want anything else put on my schedule today, unless something major comes up."

With the papers still in his hand, Andrew stepped up to the desk and laid a few papers on top of it.

"I won't add anything else to your schedule, but if I keep requesting that your meetings and appointments get rescheduled, nothing will get done. The White House doesn't function well like this, sir, and you can't ignore a country that needs you. Now more than ever. Everyone is talking about Raynetta's book and the media is still questioning what happened to Michelle. Not to mention your mother is behind bars and you'd better believe she's giving people an earful. Sam is having a difficult time in the Press Briefing Room, trying to keep up with questions being thrown at him. At some point, you need to schedule an interview and explain all of this. None of this is going away, and its best that you deal with it now, rather than later."

I yawned again and sat up straight.

"Yet again, Andrew, we're not on the same page. Sam is paid to speak on behalf of the White House and explain shit as best as he can. If he can't handle the job, then as my chief of staff, you should consider giving his job to someone else. There are a lot of females within this administration who would love to stand at that podium and tell it like it is to the media. If you think it's time to replace Sam then do it."

"I'm not talking about replacing Sam. I'm just telling you how difficult his job has been. Besides, he's loyal to you. You're not going to find a better person to take charge of that position."

I opened my arms and shrugged. "No one is loyal to me, not even you. But that's just my opinion, so tell me, again, why we're having this conversation? I believe Sam is the man for the job. And if you also believe that to be true, then let's not discuss how difficult his job is anymore. Meanwhile, you can scrap any ideas about me sitting down to do an interview. I'm not saying anything about Michelle, Raynetta, my mother . . . no one. If it doesn't pertain to moving this country forward, my lips are sealed. Also, unless I ask, I don't want to hear you talk about or make suggestions that relate to my personal life. In that department, you're known for giving shitty advice."

Andrew laughed. "I'm not going to stand here and have another one of those loyalty conversations with you, but I will say you're in denial. You may not hear about your personal issues from me, but you will hear about them from the American people. The first lady conducted an interview on the Morning Show. Things got pretty heated when Chanel Hamilton arrived. Everyone is talking about it, and from my point of view, it's embarrassing. I'm just giving you a heads up, in case you're questioned about it."

While cocking my neck from side-to-side, I gazed at Andrew through narrowed eyes. "For the last time, Andrew, I don't give a damn what the first lady does. I don't care about what happens to my mother, and with a two-million-dollar, cash only bond, she will stay exactly where she needs to be. Now please go do as I asked. Call Senator Wilson, talk to Sam and make sure no one is late for our meeting today."

Andrew nodded. He made his way to the door, but before he reached it I spoke out again. "Just so you know, I'm trying to get my mojo back. Pray for me and thanks for everything. Even your, uh, loyalty."

Andrew responded without turning around. "Mr. President, I always pray for you and loyal I am. You'll be back to being your old self in no time, and you can start by cleaning yourself up or getting in a little exercise."

"I'll be petty and recommend the same for you."

We both laughed, and after he left, I went to the Executive Residence to shower and change clothes. Trying to take Andrew's advice, I put on a navy tailored suit, trimmed my facial hair, brushed my waves and moisturized my chocolate skin. The outside of me looked pretty damn good. The inside was a mess. My heart was still heavy, and no matter how hard I tried to shake my thoughts of what had happened to Michelle, I couldn't. At times, it all seemed like a dream I would soon wake up from.

I left the Master Suite with my head hanging low. When I'd heard Raynetta conversing with someone, I moved in her direction. She stood by the Yellow Room with her arms folded. The mustard-colored pantsuit she had on hugged her curves and meshed well with her caramel skin. Her curly hair flowed midway down her back, and I couldn't help but notice she was still wearing her wedding ring. I hadn't paid much attention to it during the interview, but the three-carat sparkling ring was there.

I hadn't worn my ring, simply because I wasn't going to pretend I was committed to or still in love with a woman who had robbed me of my happiness and stabbed me in the back. Time and time again she had done it. This time was no different from the others.

"I want this whole floor spotless," Raynetta ordered as she spoke to one of the housekeepers. "The president and I rarely spend any time in the Executive Residence. There is no reason for dust to be on those tables."

"I agree and we will get on it right away," Mattie said. "Is there anything else I can get for you?"

"Not right now. Just take care of the things I mentioned and everything should be fine."

When Raynetta turned around, she bumped right into me. She took a few steps back to check me out.

"Well, well, well," she said. "The dead has arisen. What do we have here? I haven't seen you polished like this in weeks. You must have a date later."

"I don't go on dates, nor do I conduct interviews."

Raynetta snapped her fingers. "That's right. You don't, but I do. I have, at least, ten or twelve of them before the week is over. I'm enjoying myself too, and I finally had a chance to put Chanel Hamilton in her place today. You should've seen her reaction. I'm sorry if you missed, but just so you know, it was priceless."

"No, actually, it was stupid. How low are you planning to go, Raynetta? You're out there making a fool of yourself and no one cares about my intimate encounters with Chanel Hamilton. She's old news. Been there, done that and I already admitted what happened between us. I can't believe you're in need of this much attention. The way you're putting yourself out there is ridiculous."

Raynetta's smile widened as she moved her head from side-to-side.

"I'll tell you what," she said. "Meet me in my office in about thirty minutes. At that time, I'll tell you what's ridiculous. Right now, I need to go change clothes and get ready for my next book signing. We're expecting hundreds of people. I don't want to be late."

She stepped around me and made her way to the Master Suite. I didn't have thirty minutes to waste, so I hurried to my staff meeting that went on for nearly two hours. It was a productive meeting for sure. We were making plans to tackle our immigration laws, and as I had promised many congressional leaders, our judicial system had to get fixed. The prior administration had made a complete mess of things, and the whole Department of Justice needed a transformation. That, too, was in the works.

Right after the meeting concluded, Sam, Andrew and me stood in the hallway talking. I immediately got distracted by two staff members, women, who stood nearby discussing Raynetta's book. They attempted to whisper, but I'd heard everything they'd said. One woman, Lily, had the audacity to have the book hidden between a binder she'd utilized during our meeting. I interrupted Sam as he spoke to Andrew.

"Meet me in the Oval Office in about," I paused to look at my watch. "Let's say thirty minutes or so. I want to go over a few things we discussed in the meeting."

"Absolutely, Mr. President," Sam said. "We'll see you there in thirty minutes."

They walked off while continuing to discuss some of the important items from our meeting. I made my way around the corner where Lily and Ann stood, laughing and pointing out certain sections of the book.

"This part really made me laugh my tail off. I couldn't believe it. Do you think the first lady is lying about some of this? I—" Lily paused as she saw me moving closer to them.

"Hello, Mr. President," she said with a forced smile. Freckles covered her face, and with no makeup on her white skin was pale as ever. "Ann and I were just going over a few things from the meeting. We'll have those outlines on your desk by tomorrow. I think you're going to be more than pleased by what we came up with so far."

I nodded and held out my hand.

"If you don't mind, let me see what you've come up with so far."

They looked at each other, before fumbling with papers in their binders.

"I . . . I don't have all of the specifics laid out," Lily stuttered. "But as I said, it will be ready tomorrow."

"Yes, it should be," Ann added with a nod. She was a black lady on my staff who had a reputation for gossiping. "Tomorrow for sure. But in the meantime, Mr. President, can I ask you a few questions about the first lady's book? We're kind of intrigued by it and she was so detailed when she described certain things. Did you know she was going to release this book? More than anything, is it all true? I know some things are, but did the previous VP, Tyler McNeil, plot to kill you?"

I dipped my hands into my pockets and smiled. I wouldn't dare tell anyone the truth.

"Listen, ladies, okay? That book is full of lies and I don't want the two of you wasting your time on it. We have some serious work to do, so please get busy and do not disappoint me."

"Never," Lily rushed to say. "Reading this book won't stop us from doing what we need to do to push your agenda forward. I just want to know how or why the first lady would write something like this. It's, uh, well, it reveals a lot, especially if there is *some* truth to it. Not to mention that it has me on fire."

While fanning herself, Lily giggled. So did Ann.

"As I said and I won't say it again, the book tells very little truth and a whole lot of lies. I regret that the two of you seem so distracted. Maybe I should ban the book from the White House and—"

Lily removed the book from her binder. "You don't have to ban it," she said. "And you can have mine. If it's full of lies, I don't want to read anymore of it."

"Neither do I," Ann said. "Besides, I finished all of it yesterday."

I shook my head and tucked the book underneath my arm. "Back to work, ladies. Please get back to work."

"Will do, Mr. President," Lily said. "And if you have any free time in your schedule, maybe you should read the book too. That's if you already haven't."

"No thanks. My mind wouldn't be able to handle it."

They laughed and walked away. Deep down, I was disgusted. I didn't want to tell my staff what they could or couldn't read, but that damn book was a serious distraction. I wasn't sure if Raynetta had left for her book signing event or not, but thankfully, when I got to her office she was still there.

"I said thirty minutes, not two hours," she said, sitting behind her desk. "Close the door and let's talk. My book signing was postponed because there wasn't enough room. Emme is searching for a larger space as we speak or we may have to turn some people away."

I left the door open and stood close by it. "Whatever needs to be said can be said with the door open. I want you to know how disgusted I am with you and this stupid book. My staff can't get anything done because they're so caught up with it. I'm getting questioned about it and what a way to distract the American people. Your timing is off. Have you no shame for twisting the truth and telling lies?"

Raynetta got up from her desk, swishing her hips from side-to-side. She was now dressed in a red dress with a plunging neckline that revealed parts of her meaty breasts. Her colorful heels matched her jewelry and a thick black belt hugged her petite waistline. She walked by me and closed the door. The second it was shut, she addressed me with much seriousness in her eyes.

"I didn't want anyone to hear me disrespect you, but I can't think of a better time for the two of us to have a chat. I decided to put it off for a while, especially since you've been walking around here all down in the dumps. Probably crying your heart out because the woman who made you so happy is no longer here. I'm not sorry for your loss, Stephen, and after all that you've done, don't you dare strut up in here telling me what I should be ashamed of. You have some damn nerve. After asking me to divorce you, so you could be with another woman. What in the hell did you expect from me?"

The last thing I wanted to do was listen to her bullshit. I reached for the doorknob, but she snatched my hand away from it. She moved face-to-face with me, displaying much anger as she contracted her eyes and winced.

"No, you're not going to exit until I'm done. I'm not done, so feel free to stroll your unhappy ass over to that couch and have a seat."

With a blank expression on my face, I stood there and didn't budge.

"Fine," she said, not budging either. She pointed her finger near my face and spilled her guts through gritted teeth. "I told you I didn't love you anymore, and the truth is you made me hate you. You wanted me to hate you, Stephen, and once you're done being choked up about the loss of your bitch, I want you to think long and hard about everything you've done to me. You fucking destroyed me!" Her voice rose and she pointed to her chest. "Nothing, not one thing that I did compares to what you've done. It started with years and years of you always taking your mother's side, on down to the multiple hoes you continuously put before me. Yes, I've told plenty of lies during our marriage and I even had sex with a man who *you* convinced to seduce me. I tried to be everything you needed me to be, but how can I be at my best with a man who refuses to sleep in the same bed as me, plots to kill me, cheats on me and then falls in love with a homewrecker?"

Raynetta rolled her eyes and stepped away from me. Before I could respond, she swung around and continued to lash out.

"A homewrecker who didn't even have the decency to step back, wait her turn and respect your marriage. All you fell in love with was a piece of ass. Good pussy that prompted you to bravely march up in here with your chest out and your head up, asking me to divorce you. I couldn't believe your cowardly act, but yes, you did it after thinking and believing you were about to have your happily ever after. Not once did you think about how your actions destroyed me and pushed me to the point of no return. And the sad thing is, I told you exactly what you wanted to hear. I kept telling you what you wanted to hear and I'd even convinced myself that my love for you was no more. No more, Stephen, that's what I told myself."

She walked to her desk and when she opened the drawer, she pulled out a notepad I had scribbled multiple names on. She dropped the notepad on the desk and crossed her arms in front of her. A tear rolled down her face and her lips quivered as she spoke again.

"Fourteen women during our marriage, four of those women since you've been president, and you had the audacity to write those names and laugh about it. I laughed with you that day, but deep inside, I wanted to throw up. These are just the women I know about and it wouldn't surprise me if you've been intimate with prostitutes, just like your predecessors. I guess that's in the presidential playbook, huh? In there or not, I told myself no. No, I couldn't love a man like you and any love left for you would be much stupidity on my part. Much stupidity, yet in my darkest hours, my quiet moments when there is no one around but me, my lonely nights while your dick has been planted somewhere else, I can't lie to myself. I can lie to you, lie in a book, but I can't lie to myself. Foolishly, I can't shake the love I have for your disrespectful ass. I hate myself for still loving you, and the only satisfaction I get is when I step up my efforts to break a man who has seriously broken me."

Finally, she silenced herself so I had a brief moment to respond. I casually walked up to her desk and laid *her* book on top of it. I ripped a few pages while looking at her.

"You can take the so-called love you have for me and shove it wherever you wish. Good pussy was not the reason why I fell in love with Michelle, and she couldn't wreck a home that was already torn down. She was more woman than you will ever be. Don't blame her if you failed to—"

Before I could finish, Raynetta reached out and slapped my face so hard that my head jerked to the side. I squeezed my eyes to deaden the sting. My fist tightened too, and when I looked at her, her chest heaved in and out.

"Do not take me there, Stephen! I'm warning you, and if you don't want to hear what I have to say, get out!"

"I don't want to hear it not now, not ever. And just so I won't retaliate on that slap, I will get out and stay out."

I turned to walk away. Raynetta was full of anger—she yelled after me.

"One question, you fool. Ask yourself why am I still here? Why, Stephen? Why am I still here!"

"Don't know. I guess the devil in you is making you do it. Who knows?"

Raynetta growled and threw the book at me. The good thing was I had time to duck. The bad thing was I really didn't have an answer for why she decided to stay. If the shoe was on the other foot, I would've been G.O.N.E.

First Lady,
Raynetta Jefferson

I was so disappointed in Stephen. The words he'd said cut like a sharpened knife, but I had to let him know how I really felt inside. I tried to hide my true feelings, and I didn't lie when I'd told him I hated myself for still feeling the way I did. That was why I couldn't let this book thing go. I wanted to put him on blast. It was my intentions to anger him; he needed to feel some of the same pain he'd inflicted upon me. Asking me for a divorce that day was devastating—one of the worst days of my life. I pretended like it didn't hurt, told myself it didn't and I gave him the go-ahead to move on with Michelle. I mean, what else was I supposed to do? I'd poured my heart out to him before, but my words meant nothing to him. As for my actions, I could only do what I could to repair our marriage, considering his betrayals. They were bigger than him being unfaithful to me. Much bigger. I couldn't understand how or why he wasn't able to see or recognize the damage he'd done.

Unfortunately, after Michelle's death, I'd been tip toeing around the White House, trying to stay out of Stephen's way. I'd watched him for three whole weeks, walking around like a zombie and looking like he didn't have a friend in the world. Some nights he disappeared. When I inquired about it, my source told me he'd gone to Michelle's place. He had even visited her gravesite and then I was told he went to see her parents. I had no idea how that turned out, but needless to say, Stephen was a mess. He never came to the bedroom, and several nights I saw him sleeping on the Truman Balcony. I wanted to get a bat and knock some sense into him. He was right about me doing things to get attention; the only person's attention I wanted was his. I guess I'd gotten it, because right after my interview on the Morning Show he finally said something to me. I didn't expect our conversation to go well in my office, but he needed to know the truth behind my madness. I wasn't sure how long this would affect me, but the release of *Black President*, along with the millions I'd gotten, had made a difference.

A few hours after my spat with Stephen, everything had worked out at the bookstore. My signing was on again. I couldn't believe how many people had shown up. There was a long line outside the door and the inside was filled to capacity. Everyone had to clear the metal detectors and Secret Service was all over the place. I didn't have time to answer many questions. All I was asked to do was sit at a table, sign copies of my book and shake hands, if I wanted to. People couldn't even take photos with me, but seeing me seemed good enough.

"I just love you," one woman said as I signed her book. "My daughter loves you and she can't stop talking about the day she met you at her school. You were there to pass out new science books. She took a selfie with you and everything. You are definitely her Shero."

Her words made me feel so good. There were times when I didn't feel good about myself or about my actions. Today was a different story.

"Tell your daughter I said hello. I'm not sure if she's old enough to read my book, but please send her my love."

I handed the woman her book. She was near tears as she held it close to her chest. "This is so awesome. You're the greatest. Not to mention you be slayed every time I see you on TV. I wish you would tell us who your stylist is."

Never, I thought and laughed. Two other women complemented my attire as well, and they were sure to point out my Red Bottoms. The next woman in line raved about the book.

"I already read the whole thing like . . . like five times. I love the president even more, and I only wished I lived in the White House. I can't wait for the next book to drop. How long do you think it'll be?"

"Soon," I said while signing her book. "Real soon and it's going to be even better than the first book."

The women were hyped. They asked if they could take a selfie with me, but Secret Service said no. I signed several more copies of my book, and as my head was lowered, I heard the sound of a man's sexy voice that I knew all too well. Recognizing the masculine tone, I lifted my head.

"You can sign my book to Alex. Hello again, Raynetta. Good seeing you."

Without responding, I signed his book *"To Alex, a man I wasted too much time with."* I gave the book to him.

"Next," the manager at the bookstore said. "Move along please. Other people are waiting."

The manager was rude, but I didn't care. I didn't have much to say to Alex. According to Stephen, Alex was supposed to be dead. The whole lie angered me. Seeing him again didn't move me in a way he probably thought it would. And my nonchalant demeanor caused him to quickly step away so other people could get their books signed. I thoroughly enjoyed conversing with people who were elated to read *Black President*, but I was glad when the signing was over. My hand was stiff from signing so many books and I definitely needed to get up and stretch.

"Where is the restroom?" I asked the manager. "And would you mind getting me another bottle of water?"

"Of course not. The restroom is upstairs, first door on your left. I'll have your water waiting for you when you return."

Because the bookstore was still crowded, two Secret Service agents escorted me to the restroom. I shook more people's hands and even stopped to converse with a woman who questioned me about how she also wanted to write a book.

"I've been through a lot and I have so much dirt on politicians," she whispered. "When I used to be a call girl, I referred to many of them by their first names."

"Sounds interesting," I said. "Good luck with your story and don't hold anything back."

I walked away, and before I went into the restroom, a Secret Service agent went inside to check things out.

"All clear," he said. "You can go inside."

The second I pushed on the door to go inside, I heard Alex call my name. He stepped closer to me, but the Secret Service agent blocked him from coming closer.

"It's okay," Alex said then showed the agent a badge with his credentials. "I work for the president. He doesn't mind if I speak to the first lady."

Without saying a word, I entered the restroom. Alex came in behind me.

"If you don't mind," I said in a snippy tone. "I would like some privacy. I don't know why you're here. If you think I'm happy to see you, I'm not."

Alex continued to follow me as went inside of a stall. I had to pee bad, but not bad enough to hike up my dress, squat and let him watch me handle my business.

"I'm sorry you're not happy to see me," he said. "But I'm always delighted to see you. Not in a stall, so I'll turn my back until you're finished."

"No, what you can do is wait by the exit door until I'm finished. Or preferably, you can leave and catch up with me some other time."

Alex casually moved away from the stall and walked over to the sinks. With his arms folded across his broad chest, my immediate thoughts turned to Daniel Craig, 007. Alex could play his role in a heartbeat. His handsomeness didn't excite me though. I slammed the door to ignore him and locked it. After my business was completed, I left the stall to wash my hands. He stood next to me with a smirk on his face. His masculine cologne permeated the air, piercing green eyes sparkled from the lighting and his rugged beard was in full effect.

"You know I've missed you, don't you?" he said in a raspy whisper.

I sighed and wiped my hands with a paper towel.

"What do you want, Alex? Let me guess. Stephen sent you here to distract me, didn't he? I can't believe he thinks you got it like that, and how foolish of the two of you to keep wasting my time."

"He didn't ask me to come here. I saw that you were having a signing today, and since I was in the area I decided to stop by. Besides, I always enjoy watching you. I expressed to you how beautiful you are to me and every time I see you my heart does this."

He reached for my hand, placing it against his chest. Just for the hell of it, I kept my hand there and started to rub.

"Solid as a rock," I said. "Feels just like I remember it, and I can only wonder if your other muscle still feels the same."

"I would think so, but why don't you touch it and see."

"Touch it? You would still allow me to touch it? If I do, will you run back to the White House and tell *your* president? I'm sure he would want to know every little detail or do you plan on keeping this a secret?"

Alex squeezed my hand and moved it south. He placed it right over the hard hump in his slacks that started to stretch even more when I touched his package.

"What happens here stays here," he said. "I haven't seen or heard from the president. I told you why I was here."

I gently massaged his package and leaned in closer to him. With my body pressed against his, he backed against the wall behind him. I gazed into his eyes and licked across my lips.

"If that's the case," I teased. "Then maybe we should take full advantage of this spontaneous opportunity."

24

"Maybe we should. I'll follow your lead. You always seem to direct me down the right path."

I reached for Alex's hand, moved it up my dress and directed it to the crotch section of my panties. I didn't have to tell him what to do because he already knew. He stretched my panties aside and swiped his fingers against my moist folds. I sweetened the deal with a kiss, followed by another one. By then, I could feel Alex's heart racing against my chest.

"Why do you always tease me like this?" he asked. "Let's get out of here and go somewhere private. You won't regret it, Raynetta. I promise to satisfy you in every way possible."

Alex's muscle was so hard that it stretched the fabric in his slacks and brought down his zipper. I reached inside; my whole hand couldn't cover it. On the other side of things, he dipped his fingers into my haven and stirred. As his eyelids fluttered, he leaned in to kiss me, but I moved my head back to avoid his hungry lips.

"I don't want to go anywhere private," I said softly. "What I want is for you to go back to the bat cave, tell the president how good I feel and how wet your fingers are. Tell him how much you still excite me and—"

"No, I promise. I promise I won't say a word to him. Just go with me tonight or meet me somewhere close by. We have to finish what we started here and what we do is none of the president's business."

I moved Alex's hand away from my goodies, but kept a tight grip on his package. While looking into his eyes, I had many regrets. Regrets that made me squeeze his muscle harder and harder. So hard that his mouth dropped open and his eyes started to fill with tears.

"What are you doing?" he shouted as a string of saliva dripped from his mouth. He squeezed my hand and tried to remove it. By then, Secret Service had rushed into the restroom. The agent's eyes grew wide as he witnessed my hand gripped over Alex's steel. He tried to move away from me, but with his back against the wall, and with his balls twisted between two of my fingers, he couldn't go far.

"Raynetta, pleeeease," he whined. "Let it go and do . . . don't squeeze any harder. If you do, I'll have to hurt you. The last thing I want to do is hurt you, so let it goooo, now!"

I slowly released my grip, but lifted my knee and pushed it right into his muscle. He immediately fell to his knees and covered his damaged goods with both hands. More saliva dripped from his mouth that was wide open. He tried to speak, but couldn't.

"I despise weak men, Alex. And fool me once, shame on you. Fool me twice, no, sorry, you can't. I know you're speechless right now, but I'm sure your words will flow a lot better when you're relaying this little incident to the president. Then again, I just may get to tell him all about this before you do."

I walked off. The Secret Service agent who had come into the restroom was so stunned he just stood there in awe.

I returned to the White House nearly an hour later. It was almost eleven o'clock at night and I was totally beat. I couldn't wait to shower, put on my nightgown and hit the bed. But as soon as I entered the Master Suite, I saw Stephen in bed reading *Black President*. He turned his head to look at me; I looked at him.

"You're so good at stretching the truth," he said. "I'm amazed by your fictitious piece of work, and if only the American people knew the facts."

"I did share the facts and you can call it what you wish. Meanwhile, let me warn you about something before you get too far ahead of yourself. Sending Alex my way again isn't going to work. I'm not interested in him anymore, so hurry up and seek plan B."

"I don't have a plan B because I was so sure plan A would work. And if you've seen Alex, he's not part of my plan. My plans consist of trying to keep you busy so you can get off my back and forget about writing another damn book."

Was he trying to deny his little plan with Alex? I couldn't help but to wonder if Stephen had already spoken to him. Deep down, I was livid about their little game. Then again, I could play on them too.

"So, the plot was to keep me busy, huh? Why send another man to keep me busy when you can do it yourself? I guess because you could never get me as excited as Alex just did. His touch takes me there every time, but as long as he's still working for you, I'm not interested."

Stephen pointed to the book that was now resting on his lap.

"The only plot I've been seeking is the one in this book. You missed the mark because I haven't found it yet. All I've read is a bunch of bull. How much longer will I have to read, until some of this starts to make sense?"

I don't know why I let him get underneath my skin, but I did. The fact that he was ignoring me about the Alex thing fired me up. It caused me to snatch the book from his lap and toss it. As he made a move to get out of bed and get the book from the floor, I stood in front of him so he couldn't move. I reached for his hand, and just like I'd done with Alex, I placed Stephen's hand on the crotch section of my wet panties. Unlike Alex's roaming fingers, Stephen's fingers didn't move.

"I'm not impressed," he said with a blank expression on his face. "Step back and release my hand."

"I'm not impressed either, but it's only fair that you finish what you started. I could've let Alex finish, but instead of him, I choose you."

"Please don't do me any favors."

Stephen tried to stand up again, but this time I pushed him on the bed and crawled on top of him. He laid back and released a deep sigh.

"I'm not in the mood for this," he said. "You may want to hit the pause button."

"And you may want to shut the hell up, until I'm finished."

While straddling his lap, I kicked off my shoes and pulled my dress over my head. Without a bra on, my firm breasts stood at attention. The only thing covering my goodies was black silk panties that sat high on my curvy hips. Stephen's muscle rested between my legs, but unfortunately, I couldn't feel much of it. His eyes stayed locked with mine; they never ventured elsewhere.

"What are you doing?" he asked. "It's been almost five months, maybe longer, since we've done this. If you think this is going to change anything, you're sadly mistaken."

"Trust me when I say it's not going to change a thing. I'm just horny as hell, especially after Alex touched me. Like I said before, finish what *you* started or don't start nothing at all."

In an attempt to get up again, Stephen lifted his back from the bed. "I suggest you go find Alex and let him finish what he started. And like I said before, I'm not in the mood for this."

I touched his chest to push him back again. He grabbed my wrist, squeezed it and rejected my move.

"I said no, Raynetta. Get up, put your clothes back on or go take a cold shower."

I pulled my wrist away from his tight grip and sat up straight on top of him. For a split second, the direction of his eyes traveled to my breasts. I had his attention, even if he wasn't willing to admit it.

"What's the big deal?" I massaged my breasts together to energize him. "It's just sex. How much longer are you going to deprive yourself?"

I felt his muscle thumping between my legs and then it stopped. He lay back on the bed and tucked his hands behind his head. To avoid looking at me, he closed his eyes.

"Let this go," he said. "I don't want to hurt your feelings, but I'm not feeling this with you. Not one single bit."

Not believing him, I leaned forward. My hard nipples touched his chest and forced him to open his eyes.

"You can't hurt my feelings any more than you already have. The least you can do tonight is try. You haven't been inside of me in months and I—"

I paused because he closed his eyes again. His rejection upset me; I was forced to go where I didn't want to.

"Is it that hard for you to have sex with me? With your own wife, Stephen, and are you laying there thinking about Michelle? Is she the reason you can't do this? If so, then do to me what you would do to her, if she was here. That should get you worked up, shouldn't it?"

His chest heaved up and down while he kept his eyes shut. His words, however, were harsh as hell.

"You're not her, so get the hell up. How many times do I have to say I don't want to do this with you?"

"You're damn right I'm not her and I never wanted to be her. You can reject this a million times and I still wouldn't—"

Catching me off guard, Stephen moved quickly to get me off of him. He switched positions and was now on top of me. With my legs wide open, he pulled on my panties, ripping them away from my body. He then lowered his pajama pants underneath his butt, and in a matter of seconds his hard muscle broke into my tight folds like a thief in the night. His speedy, deep thrusts were quite painful. They caused me to squeeze my eyes every time he dug deeper. In an attempt to slow things down, I held his hips and pressed my fingers into his flesh. That didn't change the pace—it caused him to grunt louder and grind harder. I surely couldn't keep up with his pace, and as my body scooted further back on the bed, as a result of his fast movements, I secured my legs around his back to hold on. My insides were being hammered, and never, ever had Stephen made love to me like this.

"So, this is how you do me, huh?" I whined and tried to catch my breath. "You're just going to have sex with me like I'm some kind of slut in a porn movie."

He released one of my legs that was held high with his arm. His fast pace continued and as sweat formed on both of our bodies, he secured my hands above my head and went all in on my wobbling breasts. His sucks and massages were rough, and the numerous bites at my nipples made them sore. I wanted to slow things down, but his steel sliding against my walls felt so good that I didn't want to halt his actions. My insides talked loud and clear. We could hear the sounds of my pussy popping and that inspired Stephen even more.

"I'm pulling out. Get on your hands and knees and meet me at the edge of the bed," he directed.

Feeling enthused, I followed procedure. He stepped out of his pajama pants, and after positioning my sweet cheeks right in front of him, he entered me from behind. I felt every single inch of him gliding against my walls. The tip of his head reached the depths of my tunnel. I gasped loudly, and every time I moved forward to escape his deep strokes, he grabbed my hips to pull me back in his direction. I worked hard to please him too, and as we were now in a good place, he spoke out.

"This is what you wanted, isn't it?" he questioned while breathing heavy.

I could barely catch my breath to answer. "I . . . I did, but you've never done me like this. Is this what you did to Michelle? Did you screw her like this too, Stephen, is . . . is that why she couldn't just let us be?"

He answered by grabbing the back of my hair and pulling it. My head tilted back, and as he slammed his meat deeper inside of me, he touched something he had never hit before. Whatever it was caused my legs to tremble and weaken. I could barely stay on my knees; my juices started to overflow.

"Shhhhhiiiiit," Stephen moaned. "You feel so good and I—" he paused and moaned again.

I fell forward, causing his steel to slip from my insides. He was in a hurry to finish what he'd started, but as he got on the bed, I quickly turned on my back to face him. I held his face with my hands and stared directly into his eyes as he stroked me. This time, the pace was gentle and smooth. It relaxed us both.

"Be honest," I whispered to him. "Were you thinking about her tonight? Is that why you were so aggressive and did you—"

To avoid my questions, Stephen leaned in to silence me with a kiss. I rejected it by turning my head to the side.

"Answer me," I said. "I need to know why you were so aggressive like that. Was she on your mind?"

His strokes came to a halt and he backed his head away from my hands. "I was aggressive like that because we haven't had sex in months. I needed to feel you again and I'm mad at myself about so many things. I have thought about Michelle tonight, but that's because you keep bringing up her name and forcing me to answer questions about her that don't even matter anymore. Why do you care about how I made love to her? It was a foolish thing to ask, especially when I was trying to enjoy this."

For whatever reason, I didn't believe him. My insecurities had won again. I truly felt like he'd been thinking about Michelle the whole time. I didn't want to argue with him about it, so I moved away from him and got out of bed. The guilt I'd felt for having sex with him and for still loving him started to kick in. As far as I was concerned, it would be another five or six months before I allowed this to happen again. I definitely had an itch that needed to be scratched, and tonight, he delivered in a major way and scratched far beyond the surface. A huge part of me couldn't deny how good it felt to be intimate with my husband once again. But I knew that neither of us viewed this as a turning point, and we both couldn't ignore how badly damaged we were. For me, this was summed up as much needed good sex. I was sure he'd felt the same.

President of the United States, Stephen C. Jefferson

Along with a few cabinet members from my administration, I headed to a meeting at the Pentagon with Sam and Andrew. While sitting in a boardroom, I was at the head of the table conversing with Andrew who kept whispering things that made me laugh.

"Again, I don't know what's gotten into you, but I'm glad you're finally back. I've noticed more pep in your step and it has been a long time, Mr. President, since I've seen you give VP Bass a hug. The two of you aren't, you know, doing anything I should know about, are you?"

The smile on my face vanished. "Not no, but hell no. She's not my type, but I'm very grateful to her for stepping up when needed."

"I've noticed too. I wonder if she will step up when it comes to what we're about to do with the judicial system. I think that's when all hell with her is going to break loose, so prepare yourself."

"I would be a fool not to. Call General Ferguson to see what's delaying him. He's the only person we're waiting on and we need to get started. I don't want to be here all night."

As Andrew reached for his phone to call General Ferguson, my mind traveled back to last night. Being inside of Raynetta felt like old times, but I was upset with her for constantly bringing up Michelle. It was like she purposely wanted to disrupt the moment. Her comments definitely made me think about the last time I was with Michelle, but eventually, I was able to shake it off. Some of the things Raynetta had said were on my mind, so I made a move to the hallway to call her. She answered right away.

"Yes," she said in a bubbly tone. "How may I help you?"

With the phone up to my ear, I pulled my suit jacket back and placed one of my hands in my pocket.

"I just called to check on you. Wondering if you have any book signings today."

"I have two. Then I'm going to a school to deliver some new laptops. Along with the donation I made, an organization I work with raised almost one hundred thousand dollars for new ones. I'm excited about it and more money is still pouring in."

"That's nice and this is the side of you I love the most. Tell the children I said hello and if I could be there I would. As for you, what time will you get back to the White House?"

"I'm not sure. Why are you asking?"

I paused for a moment, before answering her question. Had to make sure no one was listening. "Because I'll be there around eight or nine. Just thought I might find you in the Master Suite waiting for another, you know, repeat of last night."

There was silence before she spoke up. "You mean sex? You want to have sex again?"

"Why not? Don't you?"

"Uh, no. I told you the only reason I wanted to have sex with you was because I was horny. Alex's touch did the trick and I hope you don't think I'm lying."

"I know you are, because it's your specialty. But whether you're lying or not, I hope you'll be horny when I get there. You think that's possible?"

"No, it's not. Not a chance in hell."

I was getting slightly frustrated with her jokes. "Stop playing, alright?"

"Stephen, I'm not playing with you. Believe me, I'm not."

"Sorry, but I don't believe anything you say these days."

"Well, maybe you'll believe me when I do this."

She ended the call. I didn't bother to call back because Andrew signaled that   General Ferguson would arrive in two minutes. Minutes later, he came into the boardroom and the meeting got underway. It lasted for multiple hours; we discussed a new budget for the military.

"The American people aren't going to like the amount of money we'll be adding to the deficit," General Ferguson said. "But we must do it to keep them safe."

"I totally agree," I replied then shook his hand as we proceeded down the hallway. "Thanks for your time. I'll handle everything from here."

General Ferguson and the other attendees went one way, we went another. Andrew asked if he could speak to me in private, so we stepped into another meeting room with no windows. He shut the door, after I walked inside.

"I almost hate to bring this up, especially since you've been in such a good mood. But your mother has been trying to reach you almost every day. I know you made it clear that you didn't want to speak to her, but I received a call from a guard who stressed how out of control she's been. Since you don't have anything else on your schedule today, I think you should go talk to her. Try to calm her down and explain to her why she needs to pay for what she did. You can have her bond reduced and you should be willing to confront her about this."

I could feel my blood starting to boil. Andrew just didn't know when to let go. "I already told you—"

"I know what you told me, but please, Mr. President. I fear that she's going to do something to herself and I don't want you living with any regrets. Just go see her. Make some decisions about reducing her bond so she can get out of there, at least until her trial. Ultimately, a jury will decide her fate, and only at that time you can wash your hands and feel satisfied with the outcome."

I released a deep breath, knowing deep down Andrew had made some valid points. I'd thought about going to see my mother, just so I could look her in the eyes and tell her what she had put me through. Therefore, I agreed to it, and nearly two hours later, Andrew had set up everything. Secret Service drove us to the jailhouse and many people couldn't believe I was there. Some were overly nice, while some didn't even speak. I didn't speak either and when one snobby, fat white guard referred to me as Mr. Jefferson, I corrected her.

"Mr. President or President Jefferson, if you would. That's what I answer to, nothing more or less."

She sucked her rotten teeth and tugged at her tight pants. "I wasn't trying to be rude, sir, but since I didn't vote for you, I refuse to call you anything other than your name. That's my choice and I hope you understand."

Andrew hated when anyone attacked me. There were plenty of times when he'd witnessed racism right before his eyes. His nasty and aggressive tone caused her to take a few steps back.

"It's the president's choice to relieve you of your duties, but he would never do that. Why? Because he knows you have to pay rent in that trailer park you live in and you probably have to support you or your boyfriend's drug habit."

The woman's face turned beet red. She cocked her head back and barked like a mad dog at Andrew.

"How dare you say that to me, just because I didn't vote for him? You don't know where I live and you have no idea why my boyfriend does for a living. I want you fired for implying such a thing. When I get finished with you, your career will be done."

Before Andrew responded, I pulled him in another direction. He was so ready to go after the stupid woman, but I encouraged him not to waste his time. He wiped sweat from his bushy brows and straightened his suit jacket that was too big for his frame.

"She's an idiot," he said as we traveled down a long hallway with Secret Service leading the way. "I guess she'll be on Fox News tonight, sharing how I insulted her and asking for my resignation."

"Probably so, so prepare yourself. Just as I need to do, before I go into this room to see my mother."

"Take deep breaths, don't let her get underneath your skin and please don't strike her. I know you wouldn't do that, but I'm just reminding you."

I shook my head and almost changed my mind. Before I entered the room, though, several women were walking down the hallway with three guards surrounding them. They were excited to see me and yelled at me from afar.

"Mr. President, wit yo fine ass, I need a pardon! Been in here for a year now and all for nothing."

"Pay her no mind, handsome. She don't need no pardon. Not after what she did, but you can pardon me for sure. I got fifteen years for a simple marijuana case. I'm waiting to be transferred as we speak. It's a damn shame I'm even in here when the white man out there selling the shit too! You feel me?"

One of the guards apologized and asked the women to be quiet. I definitely understood the woman's point. Her situation would be dealt with real soon.

The black guard to my right stopped at a door. He nudged his head and told me my mother was already inside.

"She's waiting on you. Very feisty lady. I hope you're able to talk some sense into her and calm her down. We have her locked up in a cell by herself. Don't want her to interact with the others just yet. After all, she is the president's mother."

I didn't know whether to thank him or not. And without saying a word, I opened the door to go inside. Andrew and Secret Service waited outside of the door until I was finished. Immediately, I saw my mother sitting close to a small square table with her legs crossed. She wore jeans and a light-blue oversized T-shirt. Her hair was slicked straight back and without a drop of makeup on, stress was visible on her face. Small bags were underneath her eyes and there was no smile on her face. I was surprised to see her puffing on a cigarette; I guess it was to help calm her nerves.

"I knew you would show up," she said, displaying an attitude. Her lips were pursed and eyes rolled uncontrollably. "The question was when? It took you long enough."

I pulled back the chair and sat across from her in the tiny, stuffy room that had no windows. The concrete walls were painted blue and a phone that said EMERGENCY above it was on the floor.

"I'm glad you knew I was coming because I didn't know. Now that I'm here, I guess I should at least ask how you've been doing."

She whistled smoke into the air then smashed the cigarette on the table. "I don't know why you asked me that question. You really don't care how I'm doing, do you?"

I shrugged and wiped across my lips.

"You're right. I don't care anymore, Mama. The last thing I wanted to do was come here and scold you, but do you have any regrets for what you did? I warned you time and time again about drinking. I knew something tragic would happen, but never in my wildest dream did I think Michelle would be the one who'd have to pay for your fuck ups."

Her voice rose. She was ready to attack me.

"You act like I purposely tried to kill her. It was an accident, Stephen. Had that truck not swerved in my lane, she would still be alive."

I shook my head, displaying disgust with her. "So, blame it on the truck driver, right? It was all his fault, when he clearly said you were the one who was speeding and swerved into his lane. At what point are you going to take responsibility for what you did?"

"At what point are you going to realize when it's your time to go, you just got to go and get up out of here? It was all God's plan, and as far as I'm concerned, had Michelle lived she wouldn't have been no good for you or her children."

Her harsh words almost caused me to reach across the table and knock the hell out of her. I didn't realize how vindictive she was, until that moment.

"Don't throw God up in your mess. You don't have a clue what it means to be a good woman. Michelle was that and then some. She didn't deserve to die and I'm going to make sure you pay for what you did for the rest of your life."

Anger was trapped in my mother's eyes, yet she glared at me with a fake smile on her face. "Humph. I figured you would be over that bitch by now and on to the next. I'm sorry your piece of pussy is now buried six feet under, but take a deep breath and get over it, *Son*. Man the hell up. You'll find another woman and who knows? She'll probably wind up giving you better head than Michelle did. Maybe even screw you better than Raynetta and make you forget about all of this."

Her lack of remorse shocked me. I jumped up from the chair and grabbed her by the throat. Her chair hit the floor; she fell right along with it. My hand didn't move, and as she gagged and scratched at my hand, I lashed out like a distant son.

"This is the last damn time you'll see me! I was foolish to think you'd have some regrets for what you did, but I should've known better. Your ass is evil! You need some serious help, and I hope like hell you get it!"

I released my hand from her throat and backed away from her. Gobs of spit ran from her mouth as she coughed and rubbed her hands on her neck to soothe her throat.

"I do . . . don't care if you never come back here again. You're dead to me, Stephen, and you died right along with your bitch! You talk about me killing her, but how many people have you killed? And not by accident, *Son*. You are no better than me, and I can promise you that I will get out of here. One way or another I will get out of this hellhole."

"Well, your bond has now increased to three million dollars, cash only. I've already cleared your accounts, removed everything in your condo and locked the doors. You're finished. The only place you will travel from here is to the next correctional facility where you will spend the remainder of your life."

Being in her presence was starting to make me sick. I had to get out of there, so I made my way to the door. By the time I got there, she had rushed up from the floor and leaped on my back. Her fist pounded my back and she scratched the side of my face.

"You bastard!" she shouted and pounded away. "Everything I did was for you! And now you want to turn your back on me because of your whore!"

I swung around and flung her off me. She hit the floor hard. As she reached around to grab her back, she growled out in pain.

"For me?" I questioned with a twisted face. "You did it for me? You killed Michelle for me? You lied about my son for me? You told me to shoot my father for me? The list goes on and on, Mama, and when all is said and done, you did all of it for you."

While remaining on the floor, she blinked fast to clear her watery eyes. In a flash, her attitude changed.

"I'm sorry, baby, okay? I'm sorry about all of this, and . . . and I already asked God to forgive me. One day, maybe you will too."

I didn't respond. Opened the door and walked out. Secret Service and Andrew were down the hall. And without a smile on my face, they knew not to question me about my very disturbing visit with my mother.

I returned to the White House around eight o'clock that night. I was in a somber mood, but I still had high hopes that being with Raynetta again would kind of perk me up. However, when I walked into the Master Suite, she was already in bed with a half T-shirt on, no bra and cotton Zebra striped panties with multiple holes in them. A flowered scarf was tied around her head and brown mud covered her face.

"Sorry, but I was in the middle of giving myself a facial. Didn't mean to scare you. Why are you looking at me like that?"

"No reason." I removed my suit jacket and placed it on the bed, before removing my shirt and cufflinks. "I just thought you'd be a little more prepared."

She cocked her head back and squinted.

"Prepared for what? I already told you earlier I wasn't horny anymore. It could be a while before I feel hot and bothered again. Until then, don't expect to see me sprawled out in my negligee, waiting for you with my legs wide open."

Raynetta got off the bed and purposely pranced around the room like she was looking for something, just so I could see more big holes in her panties. She had definitely turned me off.

"What's up with that?" I asked, referring to her panties.

She stood by the dresser and looked down. "What's up with what? My holes?"

"Yes, your holes. As the first lady, you shouldn't be walking around with holes in your panties. That shit is tacky."

She cocked her head back again. "Tacky? Please. As if you've never seen holes in my panties before."

"As a matter of fact, I haven't. And I'd put any amount of money on it that you ripped them to turn me off. That's why you put that mess on your face. And the scarf on your head is a bit much."

"Excuse me for looking normal. Just so you know, there are a lot of women walking around in the privacy of their own homes, right now, with holes in their panties. If you slept with me every night, maybe you would know this is actually how I get down."

"I've slept with you plenty of nights before and you've never had holes in your panties. But it is what it is, Raynetta. I'm good and you don't have to worry about me laying one hand on you."

"Perfect. Maybe the next time you come to bed, I'll have on one of those sleazy pieces of negligee like Michelle used to wear, every time the two of you were together. I know she didn't have holes in her panties and I'm sure she went out of her way to please you in every way."

Her comment was enough for me to call it a night. I didn't respond, but as I went to the closet to get my pajamas, Raynetta hit me with a question that halted my steps.

"Did you have McNeil killed or was he really robbed by someone? The truth, Stephen, and it doesn't matter to me anyway. I heard about what happened to him on the news."

I wouldn't dare tell her the truth. Doing so could always backfire.

"I didn't have anything to do with it. Andrew told me about it and the FBI is investigating."

"Okay. Cool. I'm sure the family is having a field day with the old man's money. Maybe he remembered to leave me a little something in his will."

"Don't count on it."

"I promise you I'm not."

Raynetta got back in bed and picked up a spiral notebook to write. I changed into my pajamas, grabbed a fluffy pillow from the bed and headed for the door.

"Sleep tight," she said.

"Yeah, you too."

I left the Master Suite and went outside on the Truman Balcony to take in some fresh air and clear my thoughts. A cool breeze stirred outside and the view from where I sat was priceless. I propped my feet on a table. My hands were behind my head and the pillow was on my lap. My thoughts were on my mother then they turned to Michelle. I wondered if I would've ever married her or if we would've had some kids. Then again, maybe we would've gone our separate ways down the road. I surely didn't know, but I did know that I missed her. As I was in thought, my private cell phone vibrated. I removed it from my pocket to see who the caller was. It was Alex.

"Speak," I said after placing the phone on my ear.

"Not sure if she told you, but I saw Raynetta yesterday. She was at a book signing. I dropped in to say hello."

"Yes, she told me all about it. I don't recall asking you to drop in to say anything to her. What was your purpose?"

"I didn't have one. I was across the street at a coffee shop, working on something important for the general. I saw that she was having a signing, so I stopped in to pick up a book. I've been reading it too. It's rather interesting, but revealing classified information could bring about big trouble."

"You let me worry about that, alright? Meanwhile, do yourself a favor and stay away from her. She said you touched her and you already know I disapprove."

"She invited me to touch her and she wanted me to tell you—"

"Alex, I'm going to say this and then we're finished. Touch her again and I will kill you."

I hit the end button then placed the phone on the table. It vibrated again, but I didn't answer. I dropped my head back, closed my eyes and went into deep thought again.

President's Mother,
Teresa Jefferson

I had never hated my son as much as I did now. I thought he would come in here and talk to me like he'd had some sense. His whole attitude caused me to say some of the things I'd said, and I didn't appreciate him speaking to me the same doggone way his daddy, my ex-husband, used to. Stephen had so many of his traits. With each passing day, he was starting to be more and more like him. I summed it up as being a no good, arrogant, womanizing and controlling fool. Stephen wanted control over everything, including my life. But I had news for him. If he thought I was going to stay in this rat hole, he was out of his mind. I would somehow or someway get the money to get out of here, before my trial. After that, I would hire one of the best attorneys out there to represent me. I didn't care what that truck driver had said or how much I had been drinking. He swerved in my lane and caused the accident to happen.

There was no question I had been speeding. Yes, I was. But I still had control of the wheel. Everything worked out on my end because I'd had on my seatbelt. I couldn't remember if Michelle had on hers, but maybe she didn't. And if the ambulance had gotten there sooner, maybe she would've survived. They took forever getting there. I remember sitting in a lot of pain, wondering when they would show up.

I couldn't believe I was in this predicament right now. Jail was no place for a woman like me. I hadn't said much to anyone, except to some of the guards who talked to me like I was nobody. Some were nice, but there were always people who thought their positions allowed them to talk slick and say whatever they wanted. A jailbird or not, I was still the president's mother.

I paced the floor in my cell, trying to think of what I would say to Raynetta when she arrived. I had reached out to her earlier in the week to see if she would come see me. Over the years, we'd had our ups and downs. I still didn't like her and our last conversation didn't go so well. But the one thing about Raynetta was, when it came to Stephen, she would do anything for him. Maybe not for me, but surely for him. I had to focus on what would be in his best interest, not mine. Make her believe that she would be really helping him, instead of me. She was the only person who could help me get out of this situation—I needed out now.

Around noon, I was escorted to the same stuffy room I'd met Stephen in. Raynetta awaited me, and when the guard opened the door she sat with her head lowered while fumbling with her manicured nails. My nails were chipped, hair was slicked back, clothes were wrinkled and face was blah. Raynetta looked at me with pity in her eyes. She had never seen me look this way; I had to admit this was a very low point for me.

"I don't know if I should laugh or cry," Raynetta said. "You look awful."

I wanted to cuss that heifer out, but I tried my best to be nice because I needed her now, more than ever.

"You don't have to tell me," I said, sitting across from her. "Being in here is terrible. It's taking a toll on me. I don't understand how people can live like this."

"Right. And at your age, this is a bit much."

I wanted to slap her. What did she mean by "at my age?" I looked good for my age, with the exception of today.

"I don't care how old a person is, this place is a dump. The bed is more like a cot with no mattress, the walls and floors are filthy and I don't even want to discuss the toilet. I've barely been out of my cell and the food here is horrible. I hate to talk about it, but I'm sure you understand."

"No, I really don't, Teresa. I don't understand how you got here, even though you did some hateful things. I haven't forgotten about our last conversation. You were very mean to me. Now, you're calling me like we're the best friends ever. You must want something from me."

I rubbed my forehead and wiped down my face. While looking across the table, fake tears welled in my eyes.

"I called because I need you, Raynetta. Stephen hasn't been here and he refuses to answer my calls. I feel so alone and I want to get out of this place. I promise you that I'm a changed woman. I regret what happened to Michelle. I'm glad she's no longer with my son, but I feel bad about what happened."

Raynetta gave me a hard, long stare as if she was trying to read me. I had lied, but I needed to in order to get her on my side.

"What happened to Michelle was pretty tragic, and even though I didn't like her, I wish she wouldn't have died. The whole thing is unfortunate, but tell me what happened that day? How did she get in the car with you and had you been drinking that much?"

"No, I hadn't been. I had one drink that day and I keep telling everyone the accident wasn't my fault. Nobody wants to believe me because the truck driver was white and he refused to take responsibility for what he'd done. The only reason I was with Michelle was because she called to tell me about her relationship with Stephen. Said they had discussed getting married and she wanted to mend fences with me. I was upset about the whole thing, but I agreed to have dinner with her so we could talk. We had a chance to talk while in the car, and I made it clear to her that I didn't approve of her relationship with Stephen. I felt like she had crossed the line by messing around with a married man. I told her he was still in love with you. She claimed he loved her, but I disagreed. That angered her, and as she lashed out at me in the car, I just gave up. Next thing I knew, a truck came around the corner and crashed right into us."

Raynetta sucked in a deep breath then released it. "Teresa, I don't know what happened that day because I wasn't there. But I do know Stephen wasn't planning on marrying anyone. Yes, he'd asked me to divorce him, but I seriously do not believe another marriage was in his plans."

"I'm just telling you what she told me. And I don't want to hurt your feelings or anything, but Stephen also said a few things to me that let me know marriage between them had been discussed. I kept asking if he was sure about his feelings for her, because deep in my heart, I felt he wasn't over you. We argued about it, but you know how Stephen is. I just want you to know the truth about everything. No matter what you believe, I'm really not a bad person."

"Maybe not, but you've said and done some horrible things, Teresa. You may think you've had your reasons, but many of the things you've said and done to me hurt. And just when I thought we'd gotten on the right track, you started talking crazy again. You stressed how glad you were our marriage was over and you seemed happy about Stephen moving on with Michelle. Now you're saying something totally different."

"That's because I was upset that day. My views changed after my conversations with Michelle and Stephen. He was so wrong for asking you for a divorce, and since I've been in here, I've had time to think about a lot. I now realize the sacrifices you made for him, just like I have. I don't think you realize how much we have in common, and both of us have always wanted what was best for Stephen."

"You're right about that, and sometimes I made him the priority."

"Plenty of times we both have. And plenty of times he left us hanging out to dry. Like now, especially when I need him. I know he's upset with me about Michelle, but I'm his mother, Raynetta. All I want to do is tell him exactly what I told you today. I'm willing to go on trial and let a jury decide what should happen to me. The truth about that day will set me free and I'm confident about that. Still, I want out of this place. You have my word I won't bother you or Stephen, if you help me get out of here. I have no money for my bond and I need to obtain a lawyer. Please help me. I will do my best to pay you back every single dime, just . . . just help me."

Raynetta sat silent for a while. She bit into her lip then looked up at the ceiling that was dripping water.

"Why don't you keep calling Stephen to see if he will help? I don't want to get involved and I'm sure that if you tell him the truth—"

"No," I said, cutting her off. "He won't help me, Raynetta, no matter what. He's so upset about losing Michelle and whatever I say about that day doesn't matter. You saw him at the hospital and I'm sure you've seen him at the White House. Maybe the two of you have spoken about this, but he hates me. He's not going to do anything to get me out of here."

"Just give him a little more time. He'll come to—"

I cut her off again. "Raynetta, you already know the man you're married to. When he's this upset, he washes his hands to the situation. If he could kill me he would. I'm dead to him all because he feels like he lost someone of great value to him."

I could see how irritated Raynetta was, every time I mentioned Michelle. I was sure she was glad about the accident too, even though she would probably never admit it.

"I do know how Stephen is, but if I help you, this puts me in the middle again. I don't want to be—"

I reached across the table and held her hands with mine. "You don't have to be in the middle. After I get out of here, you and Stephen won't even see me. I'm going to stay as far away from the two of you as possible. I'm done interfering and my main focus will be getting an attorney to help me win my case. That's the only thing I'm concerned about. So please. Please help me this one time. I'm begging you, please."

Never thought I would find myself in a situation where I had to beg her like this. But with all the money she'd gotten from that book deal, I was sure paying my bond wouldn't set her back too much. I assumed my bond was still two million dollars, unless Stephen had already done something to manipulate things and increase it. That was why I needed Raynetta to hurry up with a decision.

She eased her hands away from mines and slowly stood up. While pacing the floor, she kept coming up with numerous reasons not to help me. She had even called me a mean bitch, but all I could do was agree with her.

"Yes, you're right. I was wrong and I shouldn't have treated you the way I did. But I have no one, Raynetta. Nobody right now. I don't know if you can relate to what this feels like, but it's a bad feeling to be all alone."

Of course she knew what loneliness felt like. Stephen had abandoned her ass too. I could sense her getting soft on me, that was until she picked up her purse and told me she was leaving.

"Let me give this some thought," she said. "Maybe I should talk to Stephen about this and see what he can do."

This time, I let my tears flow and pounded my fist on the table.

"Nothing! He won't do anything and have you heard anything I've said? He doesn't care, Raynetta. If he did, he would've been here. He would've answered his phone and at least tried to find out my side of the story. You're wasting your time talking to him. This is between you and me. Just us, and at this point, you're all I have!"

She looked at me with a little sadness in her eyes.

"I'm sorry, Teresa, but I can't give you a definitive answer today. I'll let you know something soon. Until then, take care of yourself."

I couldn't believe when she walked out. And for the next few days, I was miserable as hell. I'd even thought about hurting myself; then again, I realized I still had too much to live for.

"Ms. Jefferson," the guard yelled as I lay on the bed, staring at the ceiling. I had just eaten a sour tasting hotdog that had my stomach upset. Had thrown up and everything.

"Yes," I replied then sat up straight.

"Come with me. Your bond has been paid and you're free to go."

My eyes grew wide. Those words were like music to my ears. I rushed up to the guard and gave him a squeezing hug.

"Thank you! Are you serious? Please tell me this isn't a joke!"

He stepped back to break my tight embrace. "It's no joke. Gather your things and let's go."

I was too excited. Thank God Raynetta had come through for me.

First Lady,
Raynetta Jefferson

Don't ask me why I did it. I didn't even know why, but if I had to give a reason, I would have to say I felt sorry for Teresa. I also felt like what she'd done wasn't intentional. And sad to say, I wasn't that upset about Michelle being in a better place and away from Stephen. As long as Teresa kept her word and stayed away from us, it was all I cared about. I wanted Stephen and her to put this behind them, but that would be on their terms, not mine. In the past, Stephen always seemed to forgive her. The way I viewed it, this time was no different. Eventually, he'd come around and probably go to her trial for support.

I had just wrapped up another book signing and was on my way back to the White House. Stephen and his crew were on the golf course today and they all were preparing for another black-tie event at the White House tonight. This time, it was to celebrate VP Bass's birthday. She was turning fifty-five and the women in Stephen's administration wanted to do something special for her. Personally, I didn't like her but I told Stephen I would join him. He'd been in a much better mood, but I couldn't take credit for it. I had been playing him off like a bitter ex-girlfriend. I wasn't really interested in having sex with him again and I'd already felt like a fool for going there the other night. He, however, seemed hyped about it. I guess there wasn't another woman occupying his time right now, but when another one came along, I was sure things would change.

I guess I would've felt a little better had Stephen apologized to me. Had he told me he'd made a mistake by asking me to divorce him. Not only that, but he regretted it. That he still loved me, as much as I loved him. Unfortunately, I got none of that from him. Nothing. That was why this was harder on me than anyone had realized.

By seven o'clock that night, the East Room was filled to capacity. Numerous chairs surrounded a stage area where one of VP Bass's favorite bands played. The music had nearly everyone on their feet dancing and clapping. Drinks were being served and so was an array of food that was simply delicious. From lobster tails to meatballs, we had it all. Her birthday cake was huge; it was a four-tier cake with yellow and pink flowers flowing down the sides. It was lovely, but not as lovely as she was. With a cream fitted dress on and a long slit up the front, VP Bass was hooked up. Her red hair was in a neat bun and curls dangled along the sides of her face. The makeup she wore made her look better than I had ever seen her, and the loud red lipstick added even more beauty. She was a healthy woman—I was shocked her stylist had finally gotten it right.

As for me, I kept it simple. I wore a metallic bronze dress that crossed over my breasts. It was strapless and was so long that it draped over my high-heeled shoes. A diamond choker necklace was gathered around my neck and my hair was pulled back into a shiny, sleek ponytail that hung midway down my back. Stephen wore a triple black tuxedo, shirt and a silk bowtie. He looked so spectacular to me, but since he was busy conversing with everyone else, I barely had a moment to tell him how nice he looked.

Tipsy and full of laughs, VP Bass made her way to the stage to speak to everyone. A flute glass was in her hand, but the glass was empty.

"Will someone please fill this up for me," she said, holding the glass high. "I want to give a toast to myself tonight."

I guess Stephen didn't want her to embarrass herself any more than she'd already had. He stepped on stage with her and reached for her glass.

"Would one of the servers please get her more wine? Afterwards, I'd like to give a toast to our VP. She is an awesome lady, isn't she?"

Many people clapped and agreed. VP Bass blushed. She looked at Stephen with tears welled in her eyes. Her wine glass was filled, along with several others before Stephen gave a toast. He reached for her hand and held it with his. With both of their glasses held high, he started to speak.

"I just want to thank you for all that you've done. When we started this journey together, it was rough. I never thought we would get along, nor did I believe that as a Republican and a Democrat, the two of us would agree on anything. But you proved me wrong. You stepped up to the plate when you needed to, made the right decisions for this country, and you've never been afraid to simply tell it like it is. I wouldn't want anyone else in your position, and as we move forward together, you and I will go down as being one of the best teams in history. Happy Birthday and may God bless you with millions more."

Everyone laughed and clapped again. As we guzzled down wine, VP Bass wiped her tears and responded to Stephen's kind words.

"Mr. President, I think you've had too much to drink," she said then laughed. So did the others. "You know we've had our share of problems, but you're so right. God will bless me with millions of birthday parties, yet I'm still waiting for him to bless me with just one million dollars."

Senator Baker yelled from the back of the room. "You already have millions! Given to you by the NRA!"

This time, only a few people laughed. VP Bass cut her eyes at him and continued.

"The last time I checked, the National Rifle Association wasn't giving away millions. They were only giving good advice that go along with our values and protect our second amendment rights. That's just my opinion, but getting back to me and the president, I thank you for your kind words. I also thank all of you for being here tonight to celebrate my birthday. Continue to enjoy yourselves and do not let any of that delicious food go to waste."

I'd had my own personal thoughts about the NRA, but I kept my mouth shut because I didn't want to ruin the party. Per her request, though, I had another piece of cake and a plate full of shrimp cocktail. As I was sitting in a chair, talking to another senator, I saw Stephen standing close by the door. He was by himself; Sam and his wife had just walked away. I excused myself from the senator and made my way up to him.

"Finally," I said, standing in front of him. "You're alone."

"Not for long, so speak before someone pulls me away."

"I didn't want anything. Just wanted to say you look nice and it was kind of you to say those sweet things about VP Bass, even if you didn't mean them."

He laughed and folded his arms across his chest.

"You look nice too, and my words about the VP were sincere. Plus, I was trying to butter her up because I need her on board when we start tackling issues with our judicial system."

"I figured it was something, especially when it comes to you being kind to people. And speaking of being kind, have you been kind enough to reach out to your mother? I'm sure she wants to hear from you."

Stephen frowned and looked at me like I had cursed at him. "Please don't go talking about that woman tonight. I'm done with her and I have no kind words for her at all."

"That's what you're saying today. Tomorrow may be a different story."

"No, it won't be. She's going to stay in jail where she belongs and I will never again speak to her. I hope and pray a jury convicts her. And the messed up thing about it is she has no damn regrets."

"How do you know she doesn't regret her actions? You should, at least, reach out to her and hear her side of the story. No matter what, she's your mother and—"

He quickly cut me off and raised his voice. "She's nothing to me, Raynetta, and you need to stay out of this. She told me herself that she doesn't regret what she did, and when I went to go see her in jail, things didn't go well. Actually, it was pretty damn bad. For the first time, I finally realized what a hateful person she is."

My heart dropped to my stomach. I was shocked by what he'd said and was also a little nervous.

"So, you went to go see her in jail? When was this?"

"A week or so ago. Maybe two, but I shouldn't have ever gone there. Then again, I'm glad I did because she showed her true colors. I apologize for ignoring you all the time when it came to her, but I just couldn't always see or understand what she was up to. I clearly see everything now."

I didn't know what to say. My stomach felt queasy and I had to ask myself one question. Had a screwed up by paying Teresa's bond? She had definitely lied to me about not seeing Stephen and there was no question she had lied to me about other things too. I was worried. Worried that she would come after him, and what if she tried to kill him? She was very upset with him, and if she caused him harm, I would never be able to forgive myself.

"Well, as long as she's still behind bars, no worries," I said, trying to hide my feelings. "I guess you'll talk to her whenever you're ready."

Stephen shrugged. He examined me with suspicion in his eyes. He could tell I was a little nervous about something.

"So, uh, do you have any holes in your panties tonight?"

His joke relieved me. "Maybe just one," I said, smiling. "And if I do, it's real little."

He shook his head. "You should be ashamed of yourself. With a classy dress on like that and looking all polished tonight, I can't believe you're walking around with a hole in your underwear. Where in the hell do they do that at?"

"At the White House, Mr. President. And I assure you the VP got holes in her undies too."

We laughed and were unable to finish our conversation because several people walked up to converse with Stephen. I quickly made my way down the hallway to see if I could find out Teresa's status. I didn't know if she still had her cell phone or not, but when I went to a secluded area where no one was, I called her. The call went to voicemail. I didn't bother to leave a message. I was so worried about this, and what if Stephen was completely done with her? Would he be upset with me for getting her out of jail? I couldn't stop thinking about how she'd lied about not seeing him. Damn, damn, damn. I should've stayed out of it.

As I stood in deep thought, I was startled when I felt a cool breeze on my neck. I thought it was Stephen, but when I swung around it was Alex. I didn't even know he was at the White House, but with so many people here it was hard to tell who was in attendance.

"Hello Gorgeous," he said. He wore a black tuxedo too, but his shirt was white, as was his silk tie. "I didn't mean to startle you."

"No problem. I was just thinking about something. Anyway, what are you doing here? Did Stephen invite you or did someone else?"

"I was invited by someone else. I wasn't going to come, but I wanted to see you again. What you did to me in the restroom that day was unnecessary. I regret you've grown to hate me, and I—"

I held up my hand to cut off Alex. "No regrets," I said. "Let's just keep it moving and be done with this. Enjoy the rest of your evening and have a good time."

As I started to walk away, Alex reached for my hand. He planted a soft kiss on the back of it and smiled.

"If that's what you want, fine. But if you ever change your mind about us, I'm here."

His words went in one ear, out the other. I wasn't buying any of this and it angered me that he and Stephen were still playing games. It didn't surprise me that as I proceeded down the hallway to make my way back into the East Room, Stephen was right there watching me. I walked right by him without saying a word. He kept looking in Alex's direction, and several minutes later they both disappeared.

President of the United States, Stephen C. Jefferson

VP Bass's party had wrapped up. I'd had a good time, until I saw Alex say something to Raynetta and grab her by the hand. I viewed his kiss as disrespect, especially since I'd told him during our last conversation to back off. He shouldn't have even been at the White House, but like always, Alex decided to challenge me and disobey my orders. No question, I had to deal with him soon.

Since I wasn't ready to call it a night, I headed to the Oval Office with Andrew and Sam. They'd had too much to drink and it was a waste of time to try and get any work done tonight.

"I guess I'd better get out of here and go find the little laaaady," Andrew said, slurring. "We'll talk in the morning, Mr. President, maybe around noon."

"Sounds good," I said. "Don't forget to handle that business with my mother. I want to make sure she never enjoys her freedom again."

He nodded then left the office. Sam and I went over a few things I wanted him to update at his press briefing tomorrow. I asked if he thought his job was becoming too difficult.

"I do, but we all have difficult jobs around here, sir. What makes mine difficult is I don't always have clarification on things and I'm left to say whatever comes at the top of my head. The media, especially the conservative media, always wants to inquire about your personal business. And you know I've been hit with hundreds of questions about the first lady's book. I don't know much about your personal affairs, and whenever I say I don't have an answer, no one believes me."

"We won't waste time discussing my personal affairs with the media, okay? Just keep doing what you do and if you ever need clarification on anything before your briefings, just ask me. If I'm not around, talk to Andrew or leave a note on my desk. I think you're doing a wonderful job. The last thing I want is for you to feel stressed."

Sam smiled and thanked me. "Get some rest, sir. You have a busy day tomorrow, and are you still planning to visit the troops next week?"

"I'm planning on it, but you know how it goes around here. Things happen and my schedule has to change. I've learned to take things day-by-day."

Sam headed for the door. Just as he was leaving, VP Bass came in. She spoke to Sam on his way out then closed the door behind her. There appeared to be something strange about her, but I didn't realize what it was until she started talking.

"I . . . I want to personally thank you again, Mr. President, for your kind words tonight." She stumbled over to the sofa where I sat with my leg crossed over the other. Instead of sitting on the sofa across from me, she plopped down on the table in front of me.

"You're welcome, but, uh, you might not want to sit on that table. You could hurt yourself."

She giggled and stood up. Instead of moving to the chair, she sat next to me and crossed her legs. The slit in her dress widened and revealed her pale white legs even more.

"I had a wonderful time." She twirled her curls with her finger while lustfully gazing at me. "The best day ever and there is only one more thing that could make it even better."

I was almost afraid to ask, but I did. "What's that?"

"You, Mr. President. Another hug from you. I'm so excited about us as a team and I know we're going to do greeeeeat things together."

Even though I didn't like where this was going, when she leaned in to hug me I softly patted her back.

"Yes indeed. We are going to do great things together," I said. "Until then, why don't you go get some sleep and get yourself prepared for our meeting with Republicans tomorrow? It should be an interesting meeting. I need you to be well informed."

She reached over and rubbed the back of my head. "I'm always well informed and prepared. Just like I'm prepared now. Why don't you turn down the lights, put on some music and let's get to know each other better than we already do."

I grabbed her hand and removed it from my head.

"I don't think that's a good idea. As a matter of fact, I think its best that you sleep this off before you say or do something else you may regret."

Her mouth dropped open. "Regret? I promise you I won't have any regrets and neither will you."

She charged in my direction and tried to plant a kiss on my lips. I hopped up, but couldn't walk away because she grabbed my hand.

"Come on, Mr. President. Have sex with me. I know you're a great lover, and according to that book I read, it says it all. Plus, I see the way you look at me. I recognize when a man wants me."

With a twisted face I snatched my hand away from her.

"Trust me. I can confirm that I'm in no way interested in you. I'm surprised you've had time to read that book, and if you have so much time on your hands, I suggest you get busy helping me draft legislation to assist the American people. For starters, let's talk about how we're going to fix our flawed criminal justice system. What are your suggestions?"

She remained seated and shrugged her shoulders. "Our judicial system is fine. There's nothing to fix, and just so you know, Mr. President, you can't keep trying to save all these thugs who are menaces to our societies. They need to be behind bars and it's important that we do whatever to keep the American people safe. Don't you agree?"

"Hell, no, I don't agree, only because your definition of a thug refers to black men. Our judicial system is not fine, and to describe it in such a way is pure ignorance on your part."

I stepped away from her and made my way to the desk. Instead of sitting down in my chair, I sat against the desk with my arms folded. Wrinkles lined my forehead; my brows were scrunched inward. VP Bass remained on the sofa, facing me.

"Why do you have to be so mean?" she asked. "We have plenty of time to discuss issues centered on *your* people. And who knows? After I get a piece of your black meat in me, maybe I'll evolve in some of the areas you wish to discuss."

I wasn't even shocked by her comments. But in my head, I had called her many foul names a man of my stature should never use. Then again, no man should use them. Not even the ones she'd referenced as thugs. She continued to dig a deeper hole for herself.

"Aren't you flattered and turned on when sexy women, like myself, approach you? I don't do this often, but I would think you would be pleased. It's not often that black men get offers like this from, well, skilled white women like me."

I hated to disrespect her, but this was a bit much.

"First of all, I'm going to give you one more opportunity to get up, shut up and get the hell out of here. I don't know what kind of man you think I am, but just so you know, I'm not interested in skilled white women like you. I can only imagine what would happen to me if the shoe was on the other foot and I approached you like this. You'd be hollering rape, sexual harassment and everything else. I'm chalking this up as a drunk woman who doesn't know better. That's how it will remain, provided that you leave now and leave quietly."

She wasn't giving up. She got off the sofa, teased her messy hair with the tips of her fingers and walked up to me. Her hand touched my chest, and as she moved it down to my package, she fell to her knees in front of me. I grabbed her hand and squeezed it tight.

"Do you think this is a fucking joke or something? What in the hell is wrong with you? Get the hell up, now!"

She used her other hand to grab at my pants. I was so turned off by her actions that I pulled her hair back and forced her to look up at me. I spoke through gritted teeth.

"You'd better—"

"That's right, Mr. President. I like it rough. Do your thing, man, do it!"

I nodded and yanked her hair tighter. "I got rough and tough for you. And by tomorrow morning, you need to resign. If not, everyone will know about this. I don't give a shit if you're drunk or not. You will not ever approach me like this again."

I released her wrist and hair. As I stepped away from her, she grabbed at my leg. I'd thought about kicking her, but instead I reached for the phone and buzzed Secret Service.

"There's an intruder in the Oval Office. I need her out of here right now."

Within seconds, Secret Service rushed into my office. They were confused, as well as surprised, to see VP Bass on the floor holding my leg while trying to reach for my package. She wasn't even embarrassed, not even when she was ordered to stand and back away from me. All she did was laugh.

"No one needs to escort me out of here," she said, standing and straightening her clothes. "I'll see you, Mr. President, at our meeting tomorrow."

"Be sure to bring your resignation letter with you."

She threw her hand back at me and walked out. I told Secret Service what had transpired, just in case things got twisted and she accused me of being the aggressor. They took notes, and unfortunately for VP Bass, this would be her last day at the White House. The timing couldn't have been better because I couldn't tackle the judicial system with a person like her mindset.

It had been a crazy night. Instead of returning to the Master Suite, where I expected more nonsense to take place, I chilled in the Oval Office. I didn't get much sleep, but the soft music and meditating I'd done relaxed me.

The following day, things at the White House turned chaotic. VP Bass was already running around telling lies about last night. I had to explain what had happened to Andrew, and my story was verified by Secret Service.

"I can't believe she did this," Andrew said while standing in the Oval Office. "We were all on good terms. Now she's out there running her stupid mouth about something that didn't occur."

"I can believe it happened. History told me it could happen, but I don't know why she thinks she's going to get away with it. I asked for her resignation last night, and since she decided to handle the situation like this, I suggest we turn up the heat. Get with Sam and release a statement from the White House about this to the media. Expose her. If you have to, release a video clip showing how intoxicated she was. Ask several congressional leaders to call for her resignation and let's get her out of here by the end of the day."

"I'm on it, Mr. President. Do you want me to cancel your meeting with Republicans today?"

"Please do. I don't feel like the time is right to have any discussions with them. They're going to be upset about the VP's departure, but she needs to go. Today."

"I couldn't agree with you more. I do, however, want to remind you that the Speaker of the House isn't on the same page as you. He will replace VP Bass, making your job a little bit harder, or possibly, causing your agenda to stall."

I shrugged and had already taken that into consideration.

"It doesn't matter. By the midterms, all of them will be out of here. There are a lot of young, energized people who are ready to fill their positions and finally turn this country around. I have no problem waiting until some of them get here, and I'm going to do everything within my power to make sure they get elected."

"We all will and you're right. The young people are getting involved and as long as they're thirty years old, they can join the Senate. I wish the age requirement was less than thirty because young people are fired up in this country. They're fed up too. That's a good thing."

I agreed. Andrew left the Oval Office and within a few hours the media was on it. Every channel was spinning what had happened between me and VP Bass. Unfortunately, the news reporters who hated me the most turned things around.

"The president is a womanizer. We know this is the case from reading the first lady's book. He just couldn't keep his hands off the VP. No woman should be treated that way and he should resign today."

A male contributor chimed in. "So, you're going to ignore the statement Secret Service released? They released a statement that clearly said they were called to the Oval Office to remove the VP. Not to mention we've seen the photos. She was lit and there was no excuse for her behavior."

The blond-haired reporter was determined to make me look guilty. "We don't know all the facts and I don't believe anything Secret Service says. They're known for lying for the president and the photos I saw didn't mean anything. All they showed was a woman having a few drinks and enjoying her birthday. That's it. We women have to stick together, no matter what. I know the VP wouldn't lie about the president making advances towards her. We all know what kind of man he is."

They went back-and-forth debating the issue. My team was out in full force, trying to make sure the truth got out. Many people believed the VP had pursued me; however, so many conservatives hated me that they ignored the facts. Nonetheless, by the end of the day, additional information leaked regarding VP Bass's encounters with multiple men on Capitol Hill. I'd warned her a while back about trying to screw me; she had messed up. Not only was she on the verge of resigning, so were some of the other married Senators she'd been involved with.

"This is a mess," Sam said as we watched everything unfold in his office. "We'll wait for her to speak to the American people first and then you can respond."

"I doubt that she's going to say anything. She's too damn embarrassed."

"Could be, but we'll wait," Andrew said. "Let's wait and see what her next move will be."

By the time VP Bass made a decision to step down, it wasn't until nine o'clock that night. She refused to address the American people, so I went to the Press Briefing Room with Sam and stood before the media. My eyes traveled straight to where Michelle used to sit. Seeing her chair empty made me feel sad. I swallowed the lump in my throat and started to speak.

"It is with much regret that I had to accept the VP's resignation today. I will not provide specifics about what happened last night, but I will say her actions were very inappropriate and couldn't be ignored. Her position will be filled by the Speaker and there will be no delays when it comes to handling the people's business. This is a disappointing day for me, and I am deeply troubled that so many of you continue to believe lies when the facts have been presented. Ignoring them only proves how divided and broken we are as a nation. We have to wise up and rise up or our days ahead, as a country, will be difficult."

I paused to take a few questions. Right away, I was hit with a question that came from a female reporter who still didn't want to believe the facts.

"Mr. President, just because the VP was intoxicated last night, it doesn't necessarily mean she came on to you. Some of us are having a difficult time believing the statements from the

White House. We don't really believe everything Secret Service says and I—"

I held up my hand to cut her off. "I honestly don't give a damn what you believe. You sound like a broken record and your talking points have been repeated over and over again. Get some sense and understand that the VP didn't agree to resign because this was all one big mistake. There are also other men who were intimate with her and some mentioned they were approached in the same manner. If you want more details about that—"

As I was speaking, all eyes shifted towards the door. VP Bass stood shamefully with her head slightly lowered and wide eyes filled with tears. She walked to the podium; I politely stepped aside to let her speak. Her hands shook as she gripped the podium and her lips quivered.

"I'm going to keep this as short as possible. The president has my resignation letter and I must clear his name before I leave the White House. It was me who pursued him, and whether it was my drunken state or my issue with sex addiction, I regret my actions. I'm going to step away from politics for a while, yet I want to thank the American people for giving me an opportunity like this one. I'm always rooting for our country and I know the president and new VP will work hard at getting things done. Enjoy your evening and may God bless all of you."

As she stepped away from the podium, reporters yelled questions at her. Very disrespectful questions that made me cringe.

"How many Senators have you had sex with? I heard the number was more than twenty."

"How bad is your sex addiction?"

"Are you getting help for your disease?"

"You owe us more of an explanation for your behavior. How many men in total did you victimize?"

They went on and on. I slipped away and let Sam handle the questions. As I made my way down the corridor, VP Bass stood with another woman from my administration. VP Bass cried and told her what a mistake she'd made. She paused for a moment to confront me.

"I'm so sorry, Mr. President." She dabbed her watery eyes and runny red nose with tissue. "No words can express how sorry I am."

I didn't bother to stop. Just kept strutting towards the Oval Office like I didn't even hear her. Sorry it had to be this way, but there were too many men, especially black men, who had paid the price for the kind of lies she'd told.

I remained in the Oval Office for at least another hour or so. Things had started to settle down, and since I hadn't heard from Raynetta all day, I went to the Executive Residence to see if she was there. I didn't see her anywhere, until I went into the Master Suite. This time, she was chilling on the bed in a teal, sexy negligee that barely hid her goodies. A smile was on her face and she was lying on her side waiting for me.

"I thought you'd never get here," she said with a wide smile. "Sorry about the unfortunate situation that happened with the VP today, but I figured you would do everything within your powers to clear things up. While you were working hard on that little problem, I wanted to do everything within my powers to clear up a few things too. Come over here and allow me to work on you."

She removed the top half of her negligee and exposed her firm breasts. My eyes scanned her sexiness, but I wasn't buying it.

"One question for you," I said, still standing near the door. "What did you do?"

Her mouth opened wide, as if she was offended by my question. "What are you talking about?"

"You heard me. I asked what did you do? Obviously, you're trying to manipulate me and make up for something you did. Go ahead and tell me what it is now, before I find out later."

Raynetta rolled her eyes and sighed.

"I didn't do anything. And shame on you for accusing me of simply wanting to have a good time. What a way to ruin my surprise."

"I'm not buying your bullshit, Raynetta. Out with it or else."

"Or else what?" She snapped. "I don't know what you're talking about, so stop talking nonsense and get in the bed. It's been a long day. You probably need a good backrub, and don't you want me to help you relieve some stress?"

All I could do was shake my head. Knowing that she was up to something, I left the Master Suite in a hurry. I assumed her sudden change of heart had something to do with Alex, so I called him so we could meet somewhere in private.

"How about I come to the White House to pick you up," he said. "That way, no one will be suspicious and we can talk. I think we need to, especially after what you said to me the other night."

"I said what I meant, but I think I've changed my mind. Let's not meet anywhere in private. Why don't you come to the White House and let's discuss this little matter in the Oval Office. If you can make it within the hour, please do."

"On my way, sir. See you soon."

I kept thinking about what Raynetta was up to. I just knew it had something to do with Alex, but when he arrived, he denied being alone with her again.

"Yes, I saw her at the party, and prior to that I saw her at her book signing. I didn't think it would cause any harm if I went inside that day to say hello."

"It is a problem because I told her you were dead. Can't say if she believed it or not, but you were supposed to be out of the picture. I just want to be clear, Alex. You play by my rules and my rules only. I could have finished you off a while back but I didn't. You've been very helpful to me on some of my missions, but I don't want any fuck ups from you. For the last time, I want you to stay away from Raynetta."

Alex's eye twitched as he looked at me on the sofa. He always insisted on challenging me, so his response didn't shock me.

"I've been very helpful to you, Mr. President, and don't you ever forget it. Your rules are your rules, yet there are some times when I don't wish to play by them. Where Raynetta is concerned, my hands are off." He raised his hands in the air. "I want nothing to do with your wife, but I will never deny how she makes me feel when I see her. Let's just say I get very *excited*."

I cocked my neck from side-to-side and thumbed the tip of my nose. "Yeah, I get excited too, but I don't have limitations like you do. When it comes to disobeying my rules, the choice is always yours. But please understand there are consequences for not falling in line. That's not a threat either. Just something I thought I needed to reiterate."

I stood and walked over to the cabinet to pour myself a drink. Didn't really drink, but I needed something strong in the moment.

"I didn't take your comment as a threat," Alex said. "Besides, you wouldn't threaten me because I have enough dirt on you to end your presidency or possibly send you to jail for a very long time. So, you see, Mr. President, we actually need each other. We also should respect each other; after all, who knows what could happen."

I nodded and sipped from the glass while remaining by the liquor cabinet. "I couldn't agree with you more. So maybe we should end this conversation on a positive note and get back to business that really matter."

"Sounds like a plan to me. And since you're serving drinks, I'll have a shot of whiskey before I go."

I filled Alex's glass with Bourbon and walked it over to him. After I sat back down, I lifted my glass to him.

"Here's to a fresh new start," I said. "May we erase the past and may you never touch my wife again."

Alex chuckled and tossed back some of the liquor. He cleared his throat, before speaking up again.

"I . . . I don't quite understand why it troubles you that I still feel a certain way about Raynetta, especially since you were in love with another woman. Also, you did have a thing with General Stiles, didn't you?"

I placed my glass on the table and rubbed my hands together. "Absolutely I did. Speaking of General Stiles, have you heard from her? I'm sure you have, especially since you were intimately involved with her too."

Alex seemed surprised that I knew about his involvement with General Stiles. They had been lovers long before she and I hooked up. He sipped from the glass while holding a smirk on his face.

"I speak to her every once in a while. She's living a new life that is far away from here. I'm surprised you haven't spoken to her."

"Nope. When I cut ties with people, I usually do it for good."

"I hear you, Mr. President. Same here."

Alex finished off the liquor. He placed the glass on the table and stood to leave. While buttoning his suit jacket, he stared at me with a glassy film covering his eyes. As if he was trying to focus, he kept widening his eyes and blinking.

"What's the problem?" I asked, showing concern. "Did you have too much to drink? I know one glass of whiskey didn't sneak up on you, did it?"

He sucked in a deep breath then dropped back on the sofa. As he rubbed his forehead, he closed his eyes and started rubbing them too.

"Get—please get me some water," he stuttered while reaching for his tie to loosen it from around his neck. "It's hot in here and I . . . I need some water."

I sat with my arms relaxed on top of the sofa. One leg was crossed over the other; I was calm as ever and didn't honor his request.

"The water won't be necessary, Alex, because by the time I go get it, it'll be too late. Maybe not too late for me to tell you how badly you fucked up. I tried to be nice, gave you multiple chances to get your act together, but you just couldn't do it. The Presidential Playbook taught me how to deal with people like you. It provided specific information on how to handle you right here in the Oval Office. Right here and look at how easy this was."

Alex stared at me with wide eyes. Beads of sweat were all over his face and while his mouth was open, he couldn't even speak. His tongue hung from his mouth, and as he attempted to soothe his neck with his hand, he could barely move it.

"Guuuu, guuuuu," he said like he was gargling water. His eyes turned fire red like his face.

I stood, stretched and yawned. "I know, man. It looks pretty painful, and the good thing is, it's almost over. At least you now know I'm a man of my word. I just said when I cut ties with people, I'm done. We, sir, are done."

Alex tried to stand and charge at me, but his body crashed on the table and hit the floor. He rolled on his back, and within a few more seconds, I watched him take his last breath. I stepped over him, smooth walked my way to the phone, pushed a button and called Secret Service.

"I need help in here right away!" I spoke in a panic. "Code three, agent down! I . . . I'm trying to save him. Hurry!"

Secret Service was always nearby, so I hurried to remove my jacket, rolled up my sleeves, popped open a few buttons on my shirt and dropped to the floor where Alex was. As I leaned over him, I pumped his chest and barely blew into his mouth, pretending to save him.

"Out of the way, Mr. President," Secret Service yelled. Numerous agents had entered the Oval Office and as one agent worked on Alex, another pulled me away from him. I staggered and held my chest as it heaved in and out.

"Is he going to be okay?" I questioned. "We were just talking and as he was drinking he clenched his chest like he was having a heart attack."

"We're going to do our best to save him, Mr. President. Have a seat and calm down. If you want to go outside to get some fresh air, please do."

I decided to stay. And within the next few minutes, the Oval Office had been taken over by Secret Service and an in-house doctor who was there for emergencies like this. He looked at me and confirmed Alex's death.

"I'm sorry, Mr. President. There is nothing else I can do."

Appearing choked up, I nodded and thanked the doctor. "Thanks for your efforts. I appreciate you, more than you know."

Preparations were made to clear the Oval Office and keep what had happened a secret. Alex was quietly removed; he was no more. Now, the only thing I had to do was find out what Raynetta had been hiding from me.

First Lady,
Raynetta Jefferson

I had been walking around on pins and needles. The more I'd thought about my decision to pay Teresa's bond, the more I regretted my decision. I could feel it in my gut that things were about to turn ugly. She had lied to me, and whenever her lies were involved, it never turned out well for any of us. I had to find out what she was up to, if anything. And I certainly needed to get to her before Stephen did. I guess he still didn't know she had left the jailhouse. But all it took was one phone call to find out I was the one responsible for her release.

Then again, I could've cleared up all of this by just telling Stephen the truth. I could tell him I didn't know how heated things had gotten between them, only because she'd told me she hadn't seen him. I only paid her bond out of concern for her wellbeing—I wondered if he would understand my reasons.

With that in mind, I decided to go to the Oval Office and tell him the truth. He would be upset with me for a while, but the day would come when he'd get over it. That was exactly what I'd told myself, but when I arrived at the Oval Office and noticed he wasn't in a good mood, I had doubts about sharing anything with him.

"You always say it's important when you want to talk," he said while working at his desk. "But your idea of important isn't always what I view as important."

"Maybe so, but this is up there. I need you to understand why I did something you may not agree with. At the time, I thought it was something you wanted too."

He closed his binder and laid a pen on the desk. While relaxing back in the chair, he looked at me with a blank expression on his face.

"I figured you were up to something, but before you break me down once again, how bad is it, Raynetta? Is it in reference to another book deal, about you having sex with someone else, more lies, what?"

"It has nothing to do with my book deal nor does it have anything to do with sex. It's about your mother."

"What about my mother? Have you spoken to her?"

I started to pace the floor in front of the Resolute desk. "As a matter of fact, I have. I actually went to the jailhouse to see her. She looked awful, Stephen. I hated to see her like that."

He shrugged and sat up straight. "Well, too bad. I don't care how awful she looks. When I was there, she didn't look bad at all. Her mouth was running and she was very clear about not having any regrets."

I halted my steps and fumbled with my nails. "But . . . But she does regret what she did. She told me so and she was very sincere. She explained what actually happened that day and what if she's telling the truth about that truck swerving into her lane? She said she only had one drink. Could it be possible the truck driver was speeding too? We just don't know because none of us were there."

His face tightened and frustrations were starting to show. "I'm in awe that you're defending her actions and you believe her lies. I get that you didn't like Michelle, but my mother killed someone, Raynetta. Whether you liked Michelle or not, a person is dead because of my mother's obsession with drinking. She looked me in the eyes and told me she didn't care. That it was pretty much a good thing Michelle was dead and she took no responsibility, whatsoever, for her actions. She blamed everyone, including the paramedics for not getting there fast enough. I can't and I won't discuss this any further with you, especially if you continue to believe her bullshit lies."

I stood still to face him. "I get that you don't believe her, but all I'm saying is maybe you don't want to believe her because of Michelle. Trust me, I know how you felt about her, but maybe you're just so upset—"

He slammed his hand on the desk and barked at me. "Raynetta! Have you not heard anything I've said? She lied! She lied to you and I have proof that she lied! I watched the whole accident take place on a video. Nearby cameras showed everything, including when she stopped at a convenience store to buy liquor. I don't need more proof, but if you do, I'll be happy to show you the video too. It shows who was speeding, it shows who crossed the center line and it shows Michelle's gotdamn body being thrown from the car! Now, like I said before, we're done. Talk to me about what's really important or go get ready for one of your damn book signings!"

I certainly didn't want to see that video, and even though I didn't want to continue this conversation, I had to.

"Lower your shitty tone and listen. Maybe she was at fault, but she's your mother, Stephen. You said it yourself that, no matter what, she's your mother and nothing would ever change that."

"You're absolutely right. Nothing will change it, so what's your point?"

"My point is, are you really okay with her being locked up? What if she has to stay there for the rest of her life? She doesn't deserve to be there for the rest of her life and there is no way she'll adapt to a place like that."

"She can adapt and she will for the rest of her life. No jury will watch that video and not convict her. Her actions were reckless and I'm going to make sure she stays right where she belongs."

Stephen picked up the phone to call someone.

"Who are you calling?" I asked.

"Andrew. I need to make sure he took care of something for me. My mother's bond needs to increase. I'm following up to make sure it gets done."

His words caused my stomach to tighten. "Hang up the phone until I finish saying what I came to say. It's related to her bond."

He slowly hung up the phone and narrowed his eyes while looking at me.

"Raynetta, I'm hoping and praying this has nothing to do with—" he paused after seeing my hard swallow.

"Yes. I paid her bond, Stephen. She's out of jail, only because I felt so sorry for her. She called and asked me to come see her. Said you hadn't been there for her and I felt horrible. Now I know much of what she'd said that day was a lie. I feel so foolish, but you have to understand she's family to me too."

Stephen's mouth was open but he hadn't said a word. He released a long, deep breath and shook his head. Surprisingly, his voice was calmer than I expected it to be.

"Family, huh? All of a sudden, she's like family to you. I don't know what to say to you, Raynetta. I think it is best that you leave, before I lash out at you in a way you never even thought was possible."

"Well, you're so good at disrespecting me so it should come pretty easy for you. I probably made a mistake by paying her bond, but I'm sure you'll work your magic behind the scenes to make sure she gets convicted. That's if you truly want her convicted. By the time her trial gets here, I'm sure the two of you will be chummy again and all will be forgotten. Goodbye and try to have a good day."

I left the Oval Office with an attitude. Deep down, I knew that paying her bond wasn't the right thing to do. But Stephen didn't know how to communicate with me. I didn't appreciate his threats and his tone always sent us down the wrong path.

Nonetheless, the truth was out and he could deal with it how he wished. I planned to deal with Teresa's lies in my own way, but the first thing I had to do was find her.

President's Mother,
Teresa Jefferson

Yet again, I found myself without a place to live and with that son of mine in control of everything. I was glad to be out of jail, but I still had so much to do. The way I viewed it, there was no need to consult with an attorney to fight this case for me. I was going down for sure. Stephen would see to it that it happened; I couldn't believe he had put his slut before me.

At first when I got out, I wanted to somehow or someway catch up with him. I'd thought about telling him how sorry I was about all of this, but I got tired of kissing his ass. Those days were over. It was time for me to see about myself and figure out how I was going to put closure to this mess.

While at a crummy motel room, I got out of bed, tucked a Glock 9 underneath the mattress and put on some clothes. I didn't want anyone to recognize me, so I wore a Nike cap on my head, jeans and an oversized shirt. Stephen had removed all of my clothes, and when I went to the place I used to call home, it was empty. He didn't waste any time washing his hands to me. And after all I had done for him, his behavior was gut-wrenching.

After locking the door to the room I was in, I proceeded to walk to a nearby breakfast joint to have breakfast. My stomach had been growling; I had lost, at least, five or ten pounds while in jail. I hated to even think about that place. If anyone thought I was going to return there, they were crazy. There wasn't a chance in hell it would happen—I was sure of it.

Right before I got to the restaurant, I passed a Catholic church that had two red doors wide open. Feeling like I needed a new start in life, I made a detour and went inside. There were only a few people inside praying. They sat close to the front and didn't even hear me come in. To my right was a sign that said confessions. An arrow was above it and it pointed to a wooden booth with a burgundy curtain in front of it. As I approached the booth, I saw a doorbell that said ring for priest. I pressed my finger against the doorbell, before getting comfortable inside of the booth. My legs were crossed, and when I looked at my nails, I couldn't believe how badly I needed a manicure. I started to think about what I would say to the priest, especially since he was taking so long to get here. Maybe I should've made an appointment. Then again, the sign said he was available. I didn't know exactly what to say, but when he arrived nearly fifteen minutes later, I asked for forgiveness.

"Bless me, Father, for I have sinned time and time again. I don't know what makes me do some of the things I do, but I'm here today to confess my sins and pray for forgiveness."

"When was your last confession?" he whispered in a raspy tone.

Now, I didn't know what that smell was, but something didn't seem right with his breath. I pinched my nose and couldn't remember when my last confession was so I shrugged my shoulders.

"I'm not sure. It's been a long time, I guess."

"It is recommended that you do so once a year. Continue child. I am listening."

"It is also recommended that we brush our teeth, at least, twice a day, but some people don't do it. With that being *advised*, where do I start? I guess I'll just say that I sometimes have really bad thoughts about hurting people I love. I do so much for them and it hurts when I don't feel appreciated. My son, in particular, is so disrespectful. He treats me like crap and there are times when I just want to choke the life out of him. I find myself planning his demise and he's always—"

"This confession isn't about your son. It's about your sins. Tell me about your faults and about things that make you feel bad about yourself. Why do you feel like you need forgiveness?"

Even though I couldn't see him, I looked in his direction, cocked my head back and winced. "I know all that, but I need to get some things off my chest first. Besides, I can't talk about other things, unless I tell you about my son. I thought you were supposed to just shut up and listen?"

There was a long silence. He cleared his throat and started to attack me again.

"I am listening. I just want to set you on the right path, since you haven't confessed your sins for quite some time."

"No, let me set you on the right path. When is the last time you confessed *your* sins? Probably every day, yet you sit there trying to judge me for not having to come here on a regular basis. How dare you judge me? I mean, who are you to say something like that to me when you don't even know me. And then to call yourself a man of God? Please."

"I'm sorry you feel that way. I am a man of God and I want you to return to confession when you're absolutely ready. Until then, have a blessed day. May God bless you and watch over you."

"Yeah, he's watching you too. All day, every day so watch yourself."

I pulled the curtain aside and got the hell out of there. I didn't like his attitude; maybe I'd try another church later. For now, it was time to eat. I ordered a stack of pancakes, two sausages and scrambled eggs with cheese. Just as I started to dive in, my cell phone rang. Raynetta had been calling and texting me, but there was no reason to answer her calls. I really didn't have much else to say to her, especially since I didn't need more money. The problem was she kept calling me so I had to answer.

"What?" I said. "I'm kind of busy. Can I call you back?"

"No, Teresa, I need to speak to you now. You lied to me about everything. Why did you lie and where are you?"

"That's none of your business. And I didn't lie to you about anything. What are you talking about?"

"About not seeing Stephen. He told me he saw you. Said you were real nasty to him and you told him you didn't have any regrets about what happened."

"Look. I told you how I felt about the whole ordeal. If Stephen wants to keep crying about his bitch, and you want to join him, that's your prerogative. I don't know why you continue to be a fool for him and why do you care about how I really feel? Besides, I only saw Stephen for two measly minutes. He didn't stay long, so our conversation wasn't worth mentioning."

"Teresa, don't bullshit me. Be honest and admit that all you wanted was for me to feel sorry for you so I could pay your bond. Had I known what I know now, I wouldn't have paid one dime."

"That's just Stephen in your head again. I like you, Raynetta, but you can be such an idiot at times. I don't know why so many women in this country admire you. You're not an inspiration to anyone and all you really are is the president's fool. Now, I'm getting ready to eat breakfast. Stop calling me, and like I told you at the jailhouse, I'm done with you and Stephen. You don't have to worry about hearing from me again."

I ended the call and finished my breakfast. Raynetta didn't call back, but by three o'clock in the afternoon, I went to where she was. Of course she didn't believe I was done with her and Stephen because I wasn't. She had another book signing scheduled, and when I say the library was packed, it was. Two Secret Service agents were with her and there was a security guard at the door. I snuck right in with my hat lowered and clothes looking a bit slouchy. I saw Raynetta from a short distance, laughing and conversing with people who were eager to meet her and get her autograph. She was all smiles; I just didn't understand how Stephen allowed this kind of foolishness to go on. If you ask me, she'd dissed the hell out of both of us in her book. I had read some of it while in jail. Got pretty disgusted and couldn't read anymore. To me, she made herself look like a victim, while making me and Stephen out to be villains. She's lucky I wasn't the one telling the story. If so, it would expose the truth about her being the gold digging, unsupportive wife and hooker.

I browsed the library, sat down for a while to read and waited until Raynetta was just about ready to wrap it up. Since she'd been sitting for a long time, I assumed she would need to use the restroom, even if it was just to admire herself in the mirror. She loved to look at herself, so with that in mind I moved closer to the restroom and waited. Sure enough, nearly ten minutes later, I saw her coming my way with Secret Service surrounding her. I rushed to a stall inside of the restroom and locked the door. When Secret Service knocked, I didn't say a word.

"Is anyone in here," he asked. I could hear his footsteps coming closer. "Anyone here? If so, I need you to hurry and immediately clear the restroom."

Through the crack, I could see him standing outside of the stall I was in.

"I'm in here, sir, but I may be a while. My stomach hurts really bad. And why do I have to leave? Who are you?"

All he did was grunt. After he walked away, I stayed right where I was. Raynetta didn't come into the restroom until five minutes later. I heard her heels clicking and clacking on the floor. She also coughed, before taking a leak. After she flushed the toilet, I heard her walk to the sinks and turn on the water. That was when I exited the stall and showed my face. She jumped back and held her chest.

"Damn-it, Teresa. You scared the heck out of me."

"Well, at least you didn't pee on yourself after taking that long leak. How's the book business going? Have you made the New York Times Bestseller's list yet?"

"Of course I did," she boasted. "My book was number one, prior to the release date. But you and I don't need to discuss my book. What we need to talk about is your lies. I don't know what you're up to, Teresa. If it has anything to do with hurting me or Stephen, I suggest you rethink your plan."

"See, there you go taking up for him again. You just can't stop looking out for him. It's a shame too, because the one thing I did lie about was how much I thought he cared about you. He doesn't, Raynetta. Stephen has never cared about anyone, other than himself. Then again, he cared about Michelle. He did love her, and I'm starting to know how much he did with each passing day. I didn't want to share that tad bit of information with you while I was in jail. Didn't dare want to hurt your feelings, yet again."

She stood with a smirk on her face, as if my words didn't hurt. "I swear I'm kicking myself right now for trying to save you. Lord knows I should've left you in jail to rot, but this is just one of those decisions I'm going to have to live with. Have a nice life, Teresa. You're going down, bitch, and there is nothing or no one who can save you."

She pivoted to walk away, but as she did, I reached for her long hair and grabbed it. I had always wanted to slap the hell out of her, so when she swung around, I reached back and came forth with a slap that staggered her. In total disbelief, her eyes grew wide and her whole face transformed into what looked like a demon. She charged at me with her fist and landed a hard blow to my head. As we tussled with each other, harsh words escaped our mouths.

"I hate you, you crazy bitch!"

"You're just a weak slut who has no business living in the White House!"

I threw punches and so did she. It wasn't long before Secret Service rushed into the restroom to separate us. Raynetta had a few scratches on her face from my sharp nails, and I felt a little numbness next to my eye from one of her punches.

"Stop this!" Secret Service yelled as they manhandled us both. I was held against a wall while Raynetta was forced to sit in a chair.

"Call my husband, the president," Raynetta yelled.

"That's right," I hissed. "Identify who he is to you because nobody knows for sure."

She wiped sweat from her forehead while evil eyeing me. "I want to speak to *my husband* right now! Call him!"

If I could break away from the Secret Service agent's grip to go slap her again, I would have. Instead, I silenced myself and waited for Secret Service to make a move. They made one phone call, and within the hour, Raynetta and I were taken to an underground concrete bunker. It was dark, muggy and smelled like mildew. I could barely see anything. The Secret Service agent who escorted us to a damp room was disrespectful. He kept shoving me and glaring at me through his devilish gray eyes.

"Get in there and close your freaking mouth," he said to me.

I turned around and let him have it. "Don't you tell me to shut up. You shut up and tell me why I'm here."

"I don't want to be here," Raynetta said in a more calm tone. "I'm ordering you to take me back to the White House so I can speak to Stephen. Where is he?"

The man spoke to Raynetta in a more sensible tone. "The president will be here soon. Until then, enjoy each other's company. If the two of you want to pull each other's hair out, go right ahead. There's plenty of room in here to fight like cats and dogs."

He slammed the loud steel door and left us in the room staring at each other. Raynetta cut her eyes at me and frowned.

"This is ridiculous," she fussed. "I didn't sign up for any of this and all I ever wanted was a peaceful life. I'm so sick and tired of doing this mess."

"Oh, you signed up for it and then some. 'I's gone be the First Lady of the United States of America' you said. Remember? And the more you keep defending Stephen, you have a long road ahead of you."

"Don't you stand there and talk about how much I've defended him. You're the one who has always defended him, up until recently. Stop trying to pretend as if you've been so perfect. Besides, I already know what you're doing. You're trying to turn me against him. You want me to feel sad about his relationship with Michelle, but it's not going to work, Teresa. I'm a lot smarter than you think and none of this is over until the fat lady sings."

"Your Mama already sung and the last time I checked she was dead. Just as you are, if somebody don't hurry up and get me out of this room." I looked around with a frown on my face. "What in the hell is this place?"

"I'm surprised you don't know. And you can kiss where the sun doesn't shine after speaking that way about my mother. Right back to you, and speaking of the pictures I've seen of your mother, she wasn't all that great looking, you know."

Raynetta walked away from me and lightly knocked on the door. "Is anybody down here?" she asked. "If so, open the door. Come on and open the door."

There was no response. I couldn't believe I was stuck in this room with her weak self. It was getting stuffy as hell; my clothes were sticking to my sweaty skin. I walked up to the door and pushed her aside. She pushed me back.

"Don't touch me," she barked. "Do it again and you'll . . ."

I ignored her and beat on the door. "This is how you do it," I said, banging harder. "Open this damn door before I drill my foot in your fat butt! Let me out of here or else I promise you all hell will break loose!"

I banged, screamed, hollered, cried and cussed until my mouth started to hurt. We were ignored, and the only thing I could do was find a corner to sit in until someone showed up. That wasn't until the following day.

President of the United States, Stephen C. Jefferson

I was in the middle of another long meeting when I'd gotten the call about Raynetta and my mother's *dispute* in the restroom. I was in no rush to go defuse the situation and I wasn't even surprised something like this had happened. I was, however, fed up with the shit. Both of them had been taken to the bunker, until I had some spare time on my hands to deal with the situation. After I had been fully briefed about everything, the following day I took my journey to the bunker once again. I promised myself this would be the last time. I had probably been to the bunker more than any other president in history, but when things had to get done, this was necessary. Oliver from my *special* Secret Service detail walked with me. He weighed about three-hundred-plus pounds and was very angry about the situation.

"I didn't want to say anything harsh to your mother, but she spit on me earlier today. Had she not been your mother, things would've turned out differently."

I listened and kept it moving in my gray tailored suit, shiny black shoes and crisp white shirt. I had an important appointment after this so I had to make it quick. As we reached the steel door, I ordered Oliver to stay outside.

"I'll only be a few minutes. And thanks for all your help. I really do appreciate it."

"No problem, Mr. President. Just doing my job."

He opened the door, and once I was inside, all eyes locked on me. Mean mugs were on their sweaty faces and Raynetta sat in one corner, my mother was in another.

"Nice of you to finally show your ass up," my mother said. "Let me out of here, Stephen. I don't have time for this."

"Neither do I," Raynetta added. "Why in the hell would you leave me in here with her? This is crazy, Stephen, and what kind of man keeps his wife in a place like this? I know Secret Service told you what happened. I wanted to speak to you. Why didn't you come sooner?"

"Because I'm fucking fed up, that's why. You're the one who thought it was a good idea for her to get out of jail. She's now your problem, not mine. If anything, I wanted you to stay in here so you could take all the time you needed to deal with your problem."

"Problem?" My mother said. "You're the one who is going to have a big problem, if you don't move out of my way and let me out of here."

I moved aside to let her walk by me. "Go ahead. Even though you can get by me, I don't think you'll make it passed Oliver."

"Like hell," she said and stormed towards the door, trying to open it. Raynetta had already been here and done this before. She knew it was a waste of time. Unfortunately, my mother didn't have a clue.

"Lecture us, say what you have to say, Stephen, and let's be done with this," Raynetta said. "I don't want to be in here for another minute. No words can express how pissed I am. After I get out of here, I really need to rethink some things. This is too much. You and your mother are too much for me."

"No, you and my mother are too much for me. I assumed you needed to spend some quality time with a woman you care so much about. She means so much to you that seeing her behind bars just broke your heart. I'm still trying to figure this one out, but I won't spend much more time on it. I promise."

My mother stepped away from the door and stood close to me with venom in her eyes. "At least she cared more about me than you did. You wanted me to rot in that place, but I can promise you one thing, Stephen. I'm not going back there. Never again and it will be a cold day in hell before I let you control what ultimately happens to me."

For the first time ever, I looked at her with much hatred in my heart. "You want to talk to me about control. Please. I could stand here all day and night and talk about how much you tried to control my life. I've lost too much dealing with you. I ignored so many hateful and spiteful things you did, but not anymore. You're done. This is over and you're so right when you say you're not going back to jail again."

Raynetta stepped forward and yelled at me. "Stop this shit, okay! Can't we all just get along and be done with this? She's out and a jury will decide her fate. Let her go her own way and—"

My mother snapped at Raynetta and cut her off. "I will decide my own fate, stupid. Not you, not Stephen, and not a jury. Now move back and keep your mouth closed while I continue talking to this criminal minded son of mine."

It was a good thing she'd read my criminal mind. That way, she wouldn't be so surprised by what was coming next. Just as she and Raynetta started going at it again, I reached for the silencer at my waist and aimed it straight ahead. Both Raynetta and my mother stood with their mouths hanging wide open.

"Put that damn thing down," my mother said with fury in her eyes.

"Have you lost your mind?" Raynetta questioned. "Really, Stephen?"

I responded to their comments with action and fired three shots that sprayed my suit and clean white shirt with fresh blood. Having no regrets, I sucked in a deep breath and knocked on the door for Oliver to open it.

"Clean up this mess for me," I said in a soft tone. "And as you already know, this stays between us."

He saluted me and said he'd handle everything. I walked out of the bunker with my head held high, yet feeling highly discouraged it had come to this.

Black President: The Conclusion
Season 3

President's Mother,
Teresa Jefferson

(FLASHBACK)

As I look back on that day at the hospital when Stephen found out Michelle was dead, I knew our mother and son relationship was done. The eerie look in his eyes was ice cold. He would never forgive me for what I'd done, and from that moment on, my life would be a living hell. When he ordered the police to "lock her up" he meant it. He wanted me behind bars for the rest of my life. He never wanted to come see me in jail, but I guess someone had talked him into it. By then, though, I was too angry to tell him how sorry I was. I didn't really feel *sorry* for anyone at that point, other than for myself. Yes, a horrible accident had occurred, but it wasn't like I intentionally caused it. Maybe it was my fault, but did Stephen have to completely disown me for making one of the biggest mistakes of my life? Did I, his own mother, deserve to be disrespected like this? He had thrown me under the bus and ran me over! That was how I felt—there was no other way for me to explain his ill treatment. If he'd forgiven me for all of my other fuck-ups, why not forgive me this time? It made no sense to me; I was sick and tired of being in this kind of predicament with my son. This was the last straw. His visit at the jailhouse was the last straw. I had saved him time and time again. But when I was at my lowest point that bastard refused to save me.

With that in mind, I put a plan in place that centered on his demise. He had to go. The President of the United States had to go. I always warned him about making me his enemy—this time he had screwed over the wrong person. Raynetta's slick tail was going to pay too. Stephen had always been a sucker for her. It angered me that after all this time he still didn't see what kind of snake she was. It was in her bloodline, and the truth was, she despised Stephen more than Mr. McNeil did. A mother knows these kinds of things, but when I had a son who was blinded by the devil, what was I supposed to do? He didn't even do enough to shut down her book deal. The way she referenced me was sickening. He wouldn't even stand up to her about that. Didn't say nothing—just let her do whatever to shame us both. That just took the cake for me. I wanted both of them to pay for the hurt they'd caused me, and my plan to destroy them would rock the world. I could read the headlines now: *Teresa Jefferson, the president's mother, kills him and his lousy wife!* If I was going to spend the rest of my life behind bars, it doggone well would be for something major like assassinating the president, not for driving drunk and killing his whore. I had easy access to him for sure. He worked out nearly every morning at the White House, most of the time by himself. There were times when I was allowed to go in and talk to him. No one ever thought I was there to cause him any harm and Secret Service never paid me any attention. I wasn't sure if I would shoot him or crack his skull open with one of those weights. One way or the other was fine with me, but I needed to get to Raynetta first. Doing away with her would be like taking candy from a baby. She was such a weak link. So after leaving jail, I decided not to waste any more time. I got busy. I went to her book signing, but wasn't able to slip my gun inside with me. I'd gone back to the motel to get it that day, but I had to hide it in a ceramic flower vase outside of the bookstore. My intentions were to go back and get it, after I convinced Raynetta to go somewhere in private with me so we could chat. Since she had interrupted my breakfast, I was sure she wanted to find out more about why I had lied to her at the jailhouse. Things changed, however, when I met up with her in the restroom at the bookstore. Her attitude set me off, after I exited the stall to confront her.

"Damn-it, Teresa," she said, holding her chest. I swear she was the fakest woman I had ever known. "You scared the heck out of me."

"Well, at least you didn't pee on yourself after taking that long leak. How's the book business going? Have you made the New York Times Bestseller's List yet?"

"Of course I did," she boasted. Bitch had the nerve to brag about dragging me through the mud. "My book was number one, prior to the release date. But you and I don't need to discuss my book. What we need to talk about are your lies. I don't know what you're up to, Teresa. If it has anything to do with hurting me or Stephen, I suggest you rethink your plan."

My eye twitched as I looked at her. "See, there you go taking up for him again. You just can't stop looking out for him. It's a shame too, because the one thing I did lie about was how much I thought he cared about you. He doesn't, Raynetta. Stephen has never cared about anyone, other than himself. Then again, he cared about Michelle. He did love her, and I'm starting to know how much he did with each passing day. I didn't want to share that tad bit of information with you while I was in jail. Didn't dare want to hurt your feelings, yet again."

She stood with a smirk on her face, knowing good and well she was hurt. "I swear I'm kicking myself right now for trying to save you. Lord knows I should've left you in jail to rot, but this is just one of those decisions I'm going to have to live with. Have a nice life, Teresa. You're going down, bitch, and there is nothing or no one who can save you."

Yes, ladies and gentlemen, that was the First Lady of the United States, revealing who she really was behind closed doors. The fact that so many people raved about her and wanted to read her stupid book infuriated me even more. I witnessed the hype for her at the bookstore and it upset me so much I'd thought about going back outside to get that gun and blowing more than just her head off. I, however, tripped and let her get underneath my skin. Instead of ticking her off, I should've been nice. I should've invited her to come with me, like I had planned to, instead of picking a fight with her. Our fight led to Secret Service getting involved and taking us to an underground bunker. I was nervous about being there, only because I knew Stephen would start snooping and find out what I'd been up to. I'd left some damaging things in the motel room, including my notes. Every single detail was there and I couldn't stop thinking about how victorious I would've been had I followed my plans by the book. In not doing so, I pondered a new plan while in the bunker with Raynetta. I'd thought about choking her to death, if or whenever she crawled in a corner and went to sleep. Unfortunately, she never went to sleep. All she did was pace the floor, gripe about how messed up this situation was and about how she wanted to get away from me and Stephen.

"He knows I'm here," she ranted. "I don't understand why he won't come for me. I know he doesn't blame me for this, and if he does, shame on him."

The spoiled rotten queen expected her king to come through for her. Like always, he would foolishly come rescue her. Tell her how sorry he was and all would be forgotten. I didn't say much to her while we were in the bunker, but my mind was all over the place. I wondered how Stephen would handle this situation, now that he knew Raynetta had paid my bond. I promised myself that whenever I got out of here, I would finish what I started. No ifs, ands or buts about it, I would kill the both of them and have my happily ever after soon. That was what I had hoped for, until I saw the spine-chilling look in Stephen's eyes as he entered the humid room. His eyes were locked directly on me, and the last time I'd seen that look was when he'd pulled the trigger and shot his father. My clothes stuck to my sweaty skin and my stomach rumbled. I kept my eyes glued to his, trying to read him. He knew something, but how much did he know was the question?

"Nice of you to finally show your ass up," I said. "Let me out of here, Stephen. I don't have time for this."

"Neither do I," Raynetta whined. "Why in the hell would you leave me in here with her? This is crazy, Stephen, and what kind of man keeps his wife in a place like this? I know Secret Service told you what happened. I wanted to speak to you. Why didn't you come sooner?"

All she did was whine—I was so sick of her. I was glad Stephen's eyes shifted away from me and focused on her.

"Because I'm fucking fed up, that's why. You're the one who thought it was a good idea for her to get out of jail. She's now your problem, not mine. If anything, I wanted you to stay in here so you could take all the time you needed to deal with your problem."

His eyes traveled back to me. The way he verbally attacked us told me this wasn't going to be good.

"Problem?" I said. "You're the one who is going to have a big problem, if you don't move out of my way and let me out of here."

I needed to get out of there. And trying to distract him, I rushed to the door.

"Go ahead," Stephen said. "Even though you can get by me, I don't think you'll make it passed Oliver."

"Like hell," I said, pulling on the door. It wouldn't open, but I kept trying so I could get out of there and run fast. My heart was racing. Time wasn't on my side.

"Lecture us," Raynetta barked. "Say what you have to say, Stephen, and let's be done with this. I don't want to be in here for another minute. No words can express how pissed I am. After I get out of here, I really need to rethink some things. You and your mother are too much for me."

Like always, she couldn't keep my name out of her mouth. As she and Stephen argued, I continued to bang on the door. If that fat bastard opened it, I was out!

"No, you and my mother are too much for me," Stephen said. "I assumed you needed to spend some quality time with a woman you care so much about. She means so much to you that seeing her behind bars just broke your heart. I'm still trying to figure this one out, but I won't spend much more time on it. I promise."

Realizing that no one was going to open the door, I stepped away from it and approached Stephen with venom in my eyes. He appeared unmoved.

"At least she cared more about me than you did," I said. "You wanted me to rot in that place, but I can promise you one thing, Stephen. I'm not going back to jail. Never again and it will be a cold day in hell before I let you control what ultimately happens to me."

He cocked his neck from side-to-side. All I saw was pure evil in him. "You want to talk to me about control? Please. I could stand here all day and night and talk about how much you tried to control my life. I've lost too much dealing with you. I ignored so many hateful and spiteful things you did, but not anymore. You're done. This is over and you're so right when you say you're not going back to jail again."

Right then, I knew what he was about to do. His words were clear. My stomach tightened even more and my heart thumped hard against my chest. Raynetta must've sensed something horrible was about to go down too. She quickly stepped in front of me and spoke up.

"Stop this shit, okay! Can't we all just get along and be done with this? She's out and a jury will decide her fate. Let her go her own way and—"

I snapped at her to distract Stephen and give him a little more time to think about this.

"I will decide my own fate, stupid," I said, not sure of my own words. I was in a bind. I could tell by his awkward demeanor that this was it. From the corner of my eye, I could see his fingers wiggling, but I kept on arguing with Raynetta. "I decide. Not you, not Stephen, and not a jury. Now move back and keep your mouth closed while I continue talking to this criminal minded son of mine."

As Raynetta fired back at me, I saw Stephen reach for his gun. I assumed he'd had one on him, but I didn't know where it was. My first thought was to reach for it and try to take it from him. Then again, there was no way for me to overpower him. What in the hell could I do? I looked at him with my mouth wide open, knowing there was no way out of this. He had found out about my plans. Damn, damn, damn!

"Put that damn thing down," I said. I wanted to talk some sense into him . . . tell him why I had planned to do this, but it was too late. Raynetta spoke up before I did.

"Have you lost your mind?" She questioned. "Really, Stephen?"

His eyes narrowed, nose winced as he gazed at me. After that, bullets started to fly. In a flash, I was done.

President of the United States, Stephen C. Jefferson

Today would probably go down as *one* of the worst days of my life. But what else was I supposed to do, when forced to deal with a sick mother who wanted me dead? I moved toward the exit door feeling hurt inside, but satisfied that my mother wasn't able to follow through with her reckless plans. I couldn't stop thinking about what she wanted to do to me. She wasn't going to be completely satisfied until me and Raynetta were dead. She was at a point of no return and she hated me for loving Michelle. She didn't want me to give my love to anyone else but her. That was why she'd kept Joshua away from me, why she could never accept my marriage to Raynetta, and why Michelle had to pay as well. As I was in very deep thought about what had just happened, I heard Raynetta scream my name. I didn't bother to turn around, but I could hear her voice getting closer as she ran after me in the bunker.

"Who in the hell are you?" she shouted from a short distance. "What have you done, Stephen, and why have you turned into a coldblooded killer? She was your mother! Your own mother! How could you—"

I swung around and was now face-to-face with a woman who never understood me. She just didn't get it. No matter what I said to her, my words would go in one ear, out the other.

"Stop yelling and calm the hell down!" I fired back.

Her body trembled and tears poured down her face as she looked at me. Specks of blood dotted her face and smudged mascara was underneath her eyes. She wiped her snotty nose and moved her head from side-to-side.

"Calm down? Really? How am I supposed to do that after what you did? You just shot and killed your fucking mother!"

My brows were scrunched inward; I could feel sweat rolling down the back of my neck. I swallowed the lump in my throat, but couldn't get the correct words to come out. Even if I tried to explain this to Raynetta, she would never understand. So instead of dealing with her right now, I turned to walk away from her.

"Oh my God!" she yelled. "You have nothing to say for what you just did? Am I next, Stephen! Are you going to kill me too? I guess I don't need you to answer because you already made plans to do it before!"

As I continued to step forward, her voice and loud cries faded. I needed to get out of there, but instead of going to my important scheduled meeting with the Secretary of State, I ordered Secret Service to take me back to the White House. After we arrived, I went to the Executive Residence. I needed to clean myself up and take a hot shower. It helped to relax me, but my mind couldn't stop traveling back to what I was forced to do. I tried not to think about it. Felt real numb and fought back the anger I'd had inside. Why me? I wondered. Why did the people around me always have to fuck up? I tried so hard to do right. Tried to be a better person, but it always resorted to this. I'd made many attempts to get my mother the help she needed, but she wouldn't listen to me. She wanted to have the final word; I couldn't let her do it. Not after all that I'd accomplished—no one would stand in my way ever again.

I finished my shower and wrapped a soft towel around my waist. While looking in the mirror, I saw stress written on my face. Slight puffiness was underneath my eyes and my head was throbbing. I tossed back two aspirin, before going into the bedroom area where Raynetta stood next to the bed. Her hair was scattered all over her head and her face was still stained with mascara. A suitcase was on the bed. She tossed some of her belongings inside.

"After that performance," she said in a snippy tone. "I'm out of here. I can't do this anymore, no more!"

I cleared my throat and sat on the edge of the bed. "Before you go, you probably want to take a shower and clean yourself up too."

She growled, rushed up to me and pounded my chest while screaming at the top of her lungs.

"Fuck a shower and go to hell! You're a monster, Stephen. I can't believe I'm married to a coldblooded killer! I would put any amount of money on it that you killed McNeil too. Lord knows who else."

While remaining calm, I grabbed her wrist and slightly pushed her back. "I've probably killed several more people, but I don't care to go into specific details."

She rolled her eyes and stomped back-and-forth from the closet to her suitcase, tossing things inside. She kept ranting about what had happened.

"I . . . I can't believe this. How did I ever get here? Why in the hell did I stay? I could kill myself for being so stupid. Stupid enough to wait around for you to kill me."

Tired of hearing her mouth, I got up from the bed and entered my closet. After pulling out a file with classified information inside, I dropped it on the bed next to her suitcase.

"As your president, I'm not supposed to share this kind of information with you. But since you think I'm such a horrible person, why not share? Whenever you get a chance, I want you to go through that file. You'll be able to see my mother's detailed plans for us. How she was going to shoot you at your book signing or slice your fucking throat. How she was going to come right into the Oval Office and shoot me in the head as I sat behind my desk. Possibly even attack me in my workout room. You'll be able to see what McNeil wanted to do to me and you'll finally learn how much he truly hated me. I could go on and on, but what's in that file will speak for itself. The one thing I must do as president is protect the American people. And the one thing I will always do is protect myself first. I don't give a damn who comes after me. I will always protect myself first and protect you too."

I made my way to the door, but halted my steps when she spoke up.

"You didn't protect my heart, did you? And how do I know you didn't just make up what's in that file? You've lied so much. I don't know what to believe anymore."

"Fact one, no matter where my heart was, I still protected you. Fact two, I don't have to make up anything when it comes to my enemies. And fact three is, you can believe what you want. If you don't believe anything inside of that file, close it, continue to pack and feel free to get the hell out of here. The choice has always been yours."

I went into the Yellow Room to chill. It was very peaceful and quiet. Fire was crackling in the fireplace and the silk, wingback chair I sat in was comfortable and looked fit for a king. At this point, I didn't have many regrets. I knew what had to be done and there was no need for me to look back and try to convince myself there were other options. The one thing I knew was my mother was clever. Putting her in a mental institution didn't work. Sending her to rehab didn't work. Talking to her definitely didn't—I predicted this day would come. It all boiled down to her life or mine.

I sat back and shut my eyes. After fading for what seemed like an hour or so, I was awakened by someone's touch on my chest. When I looked up, I saw Raynetta. She was calmer but tears continued to stream down her face.

"Forgive me," she said in a soft whisper. She got on her knees and reached for my hands to hold them. "I . . . I didn't know, Stephen. I just didn't want to believe your mother could be that cruel and I'm so sorry for paying her bond so she could get out of jail. Had I not done so, maybe this wouldn't have happened. I know you're disturbed by all of this and I regret not staying out of it." She paused and swallowed. I guess she was waiting for me to respond, but I hadn't. "I hate to sound foolish, because I knew how much McNeil hated you. I always knew he would try to kill you again, but I guess I ignored so many things. I feel so numb right now and foolish—"

I released my hand from hers and placed two fingers over her lips to silence her.

"It's done. It's over and now we move on. Tell no one what you read in that file and if you ever put classified information in a book, there will be consequences."

Raynetta slowly nodded. She laid her head on my lap and didn't say another word.

First Lady,
Raynetta Jefferson

The next morning, I turned in bed and reached for Stephen. He wasn't there. I quickly sat up, thinking about all that had happened. I was still on edge. All I could say was no one, not one single person, wanted to trade their life for mine. From the outside looking in, being the first lady probably looked easy. Many people assumed all I had to do was put on fancy clothes, attend numerous functions, contribute to humanitarian projects and be by my husband's side when called upon. It required so much more than that, and last night I truly felt like I had lost my mind. I had concluded this was all over with for me. To witness what my husband had done to his own mother was the biggest shock of my life. Nothing or no one could ever convince me it was the right thing to do, until I saw what was in that file. The FBI had been keeping their eyes on Teresa. They knew her every move. She had made too many threats; threats she intended to follow through on. In her motel room was cut-up photos of me and Stephen. She had scribbled horrible words across my face. I couldn't believe she was going to kill me first, and then was going to turn herself in and boast about assassinating her own son. Crazy, yes she was. But I never thought she was *that* crazy. I just didn't know the severity of her problems, but what was in that file couldn't be questioned. I was relieved Stephen had shown it to me. It was definitely information I could use in my next book, but as he'd said, there would be consequences of telling it all. Thinking about the deadline for my next book, I reached for my cell phone to call my agent.

"Hello, Raynetta," she said, seemingly in a good mood. "I hope you're having a wonderful day. Any signings schedule for this week?"

"Yes. I have plenty, but that's what I called to talk to you about. I was thinking about calling my publicist to have her cancel my upcoming signings. I also need to let you know that I don't think I'm going to submit another manuscript to you. This is really taking a toll on me and the president is highly upset about it."

She released a deep sigh. "We already knew he was going to be upset about it, so what's the big deal? Besides, you can't renege on this book deal again. You've been paid a sizeable advancement and the publisher will sue, if you don't follow through."

"I know exactly what the contract says, but you don't understand—"

"There's nothing for me to understand." Her tone went up a notch. "I went to hell and back for you, Raynetta. You have to finish your series. The American people are waiting for the next installment. They're going to be highly disappointed if they don't get it. Not to mention how the publisher is going to react."

"None of that matters to me. What matters is how I feel. And I feel as if I shouldn't write another book."

"Well, what if I have someone ghostwrite it? All you'll have to do is—"

"No. I don't want to work with a ghostwriter. Nobody knows my story but me. I'm sorry if you don't understand and I know this may cause you to lose out on a substantial amount of money. If I change my mind, I'll be in touch."

"This is bullshit, Raynetta. I—"

Not wanting to hear another word from her, I hit the end button on the phone. Changing my mind about completing the series was just a start. I had more work to do, and my only focus right now was on Stephen.

The following week, things were quiet. Stephen had been overseas with the troops, but was on his way back tomorrow. I loved watching him do his thing on TV, and I had only spoken to him twice since he'd been gone. I purposely avoided lengthy conversations with him, because I still felt some kind of way about helping Teresa get out of jail. I hoped Stephen had forgiven me, but whenever it came to me trying to figure out his feelings about things, I wasn't always so sure. Nonetheless, I kept myself busy by getting involved in numerous Humanitarian projects. From feeding the homeless to helping build new homes, my assistant Emme and I were there. She teased me about not having any scheduled book signings. So did Senator Ingram who was working on a housing project with us.

"I had high hopes for part two," Senator Ingram said. She was a black woman who had full support from the majority of her constituents. "I can't believe there will be no follow up. Are you sure you won't change your mind?"

I hammered a nail into a piece of wood. Emme and I were building some shelves.

"Nope. I'm pleased you enjoyed the first part, but there won't be a follow up. Sorry, but the writing process became too hectic for me."

"I can only imagine," Senator Ingram said. "But if you ever change your mind, I'll be waiting."

We all laughed. Less than an hour later, the shelves were done and secured against the wall. The media had arrived and started to question us about the project. Senator Ingram gave her spill about how she wanted to help low income families in the community. I was asked why I'd gotten involved, but just as I got ready to answer, I started feeling dizzy. I wiped my hand across my sweaty forehead and licked my dry lips.

"I'm involved because it . . . it's important for us to—"

I paused because the room had started to spin. My eyes watered and with numerous cameras flashing, I couldn't keep my balance. The next thing I knew, Emme grabbed me and so did Secret Service, before I hit the floor.

A few hours later, I struggled to open my eyes. My eyelids fluttered and my vision was blurred. I kept blinking, and when I was finally able to focus I saw Stephen standing by the window, gazing outside. A nurse was at the foot of the bed, smiling at me. I was in the Master Suite with a rag across my forehead. My pink nightgown was on, body was a little sore.

"Wha . . . What happened to me?" I said softly.

Stephen turned to look at me. The nurse came closer. "I'll let you and the president talk. Be sure to take your medicine on the nightstand, and if you need something else to drink, ring one of the servers. Feel free to call me too."

Stephen thanked the nurse and locked the door behind her after she walked out. The way he looked at me with so much seriousness in his eyes scared me.

"Why didn't she tell me what happened to me today?" I asked. "Am I going to be okay?"

Stephen sat sideways on the bed and released a deep breath. "Hopefully, you're going to be fine. You're pregnant, Raynetta. I hate to ask you this, but is the baby mine?"

His words were like a double . . . triple shock to me. I slowly sat up and looked at him with my mouth hanging wide open.

"Pregnant? And no you didn't just ask me that, did you?"

"Unfortunately, I had to. You're the one who told me how much Alex excites you and how he makes you feel. I don't know if you've had sex with him, but I do know that we've only had sex one time in the past four or five months."

I was trying to process all of this as fast as I could. My emotions were on the brink of running over; I was trying my best to control myself. *Pregnant?* I thought while feeling so confused, yet sure of who the father was.

"You can be such an asshole at times. Since I'm such a whore who has slept with multiple men during our marriage, maybe we should start with a paternity test. Then again, it doesn't matter who the father is, Stephen. I already know what I have to do."

"I never said you were a whore and I didn't accuse you of having sex with multiple men. I just asked about Alex. Have you had sex with him and what do you mean by you already know what you have to do?"

I was so taken aback by his questions. This was messed up and even though I knew things between us were bad, I didn't know how bad until now.

"Why are you asking me if I had sex with him? Don't you know if I did or didn't? You know everything else that goes on, and I'm sure you have ways of finding out everything you want to know. As a matter of fact, why don't you go ask Alex? He'll tell you if we had sex or not."

"Why do I have to ask Alex when you're sitting right here? I don't know why you're offended by my question. It's a legitimate question, considering what we've been through."

I snatched the sheet off me and quickly stood up. I still felt a little dizzy, but I needed to move away from Stephen. His comments truly upset me. I sat in a chair and massaged my forehead. Now that I had some leverage over him, I had to use this situation to my benefit.

"Yes, we've been through a lot," I said. "And you know what, Stephen, you're right. You have every right to question me because I did have sex with Alex. This is most likely his child, but no worries because no one will ever know about this pregnancy. Especially, not him."

Stephen sat silent for a while, staring at me. I didn't have a clue what was on his mind, but as for me, I was still stunned. I knew damn well this child was his. For him to assume anything else was gut-wrenching.

"So, uh, when did you stop taking your birth control pills? And is this something you planned with Alex?"

My mouth dropped open again. If there was a shoe nearby, I would've thrown it at him.

"I stopped taking my pills months ago, because I wasn't having sex with anyone. No Alex and I didn't plan this, and neither did you and me. We couldn't, because you were too busy with Michelle, remember?"

Every time I mentioned her name, it touched a nerve in him. His voice went up a notch.
"What in the hell does Michelle have to do with you being knocked up by Alex?"

My blood started to boil; I couldn't hold back on him any longer.

"Not a damn thing, because this baby isn't Alex's. I haven't been intimate with him in a very long time. This child is yours, Stephen, but as I clearly stated—"

He pounded his fist on the bed and raised his voice again. "Stop playing games with this shit, Raynetta! Whose baby is it? Did you have sex with him or didn't you? This is a serious matter and your lies will backfire!"

My heart raced as I got up from the chair and stood in front of him. My eyes were without a blink and much seriousness was on display.

"You're so right, Stephen, this is no game. Therefore, how can you sit there and assume something like that? If I'd been intimate with Alex, you would have known all about it, down to every single detail. Like me, you have a good idea when our baby was conceived, but for the last time, it doesn't matter."

"Is does matter. It matters a lot, and for the last time, I asked because I wanted to be sure."

"The one thing I'm sure of is this. I will never bring a child into an unstable situation like this. Into a world where daddy doesn't have time for no one and he wasn't even excited about me having a child. I swear you are so cruel. Being the president has made you numb, and with every day that passes, I'm learning so much more about the man I still refer to as my husband."

I turned to walk away, but Stephen reached for my hand and pulled me closer to him.

"Listen, okay? I'm sorry you took offense to me questioning you about Alex, but I needed to know the truth. I know you were involved with him and I had no idea if you kept seeing him or not. Maybe I shouldn't have asked, but under the circumstances, it's best to put all the cards on the table and get it out of the way now. I know our situation is fucked up and having a child won't solve our problems. And no matter what I sit here and say tonight, I know you, Raynetta. You're going to make excuses about why you don't want to be a mother and you're going to go behind my back and terminate your pregnancy. Then we'll be right back where we started, arguing, disagreeing about everything and blaming each other for this and that. We have to get on the same page. Maybe this is a chance for us to do just that."

I released my hand from his, but remained in front of him. "I like the idea of us being on the same page, so answer this for me, Stephen. Do you still love me? I already told you how I felt. Whether you believe me or not, it's the truth. Thing is, you never revealed your true feelings to me. I need to know. Now would be the perfect time for you to tell it like it is."

There was a long silence before he finally opened his mouth. I could see how he was trying to find the right words to say.

"I . . . I don't know what my feelings have to do with us having a child and it would be a shame for you to base—"

"Answer my question. I need to know. Do you still love me?"

He sighed and shifted his eyes to the left. Swallowed and couldn't even look at me when he said it.

"No, I don't. I fell out of love with you many months ago, but it doesn't mean I no longer care about you. I do. A lot, but I just don't feel like I used to feel about us."

His honesty didn't surprise me, but his words were like a hard punch to my stomach. I had to be one sick bitch to stay with Stephen. No one was keeping me here but me.

"Thanks for being honest," I said in a calm tone. "That's what I needed to know."

I walked off and went into the bathroom. After I closed the door, I leaned against it and secured my arms around my waist. My thoughts turned to how much I loved him, yet hated him too. I didn't want to be pregnant with his child. Tears filled my eyes; I tried to hold in everything by muffling my lips. Minutes later, he knocked on the door.

"Open the door, Raynetta."

I wiped my eyes and cleared my clogged throat. "I'm getting ready to take a shower. Do you need something?"

"Yes, I do. Open the door."

"Can't you wait? I won't be long. Give me fifteen or twenty minutes."

"I can't wait. Please open the door."

I hurried to wipe my eyes again then reached for the lights to dim them. As soon as I opened the door, Stephen stepped inside. Without saying a word, he looked at me and opened his arms. I moved my head from side-to-side.

"I'm okay. I just need to—"

I paused and started to walk away. I didn't get far because he reached for my arm and pulled me into his arms. My head was against his chest, my eyes were closed tight.

"I know it's bad," he said in a soft whisper. "But we have an opportunity to change things around, right here and right now."

I didn't respond. If he thought a baby was going to save us, he needed to think again.

President of the United States, Stephen C. Jefferson

After all that had been going on, the last thing I would've ever predicted was Raynetta getting pregnant. When the nurse confirmed it, I was shocked. I didn't really know if Raynetta had been with Alex or not, but after our conversation I believed she hadn't. It wasn't like I could question him about it. He was no longer around and that was a good thing. The bad thing was I didn't trust Raynetta. Didn't trust her to keep our child; didn't trust her period. She hadn't said much about the baby and she made me promise not to tell anyone. I told her I wouldn't, and I also told her how much I wanted this baby. She didn't seem to care much about what I wanted, but I was trying my best to be there for her.

Since VP Bass had resigned as Vice President, the new VP had been sworn in. Luke Janson took over and after my morning Intel briefing, I had a meeting with him. It didn't go well. Like VP Bass had done, Luke wanted to set the agenda. I wasn't comfortable with many of the Republican ideas, yet I was willing to hear him out and do my best to meet him in the middle, if I had to. He rejected all of my ideas, so I was back to square one. I understood, very well, what the first black president had been through.

"Mr. Janson," I said as we sat in the Oval Office with Andrew and Sam. "You're just another old white man who needs to retire. This country is moving in another direction, and to be quite honest with you, your days of working for lobbyists, kissing the NRA's ass and collecting a sizeable paycheck for doing nothing are over. I don't care if none of my legislation gets pushed through. Come November, the midterms are going to be a whole new ballgame. So will the next presidential election. Every time I think about it, I get overly excited."

With a wrinkled sagging face and a shiny bald spot on top of his head, he grunted and pointed his shaky finger at me.

"And you, sir, are just a confused nigger who will never see a second term. The American people have had enough of you. The Republican Party is going to make a comeback, and as you know, we always stick together. You and those damn Liberals will be out of here. The Progressives are done. I can promise you that, so prepare yourself for what's to come. You won't have any more accomplishments to celebrate on my watch." He tapped his watch and grinned. "As long as I'm the VP, your agenda items have officially stalled."

Feeling like his words were set in stone, he got up and walked out. I wanted to shove my foot up his ass, but Andrew had already prepared me for his reaction.

"I hate when that kind of language is used," Andrew said, shaking his head. "I knew the two of you would never get along, but speaking to each other that way is ridiculous."

"I agree," Sam added. "It's going to be one hell of a year, and unfortunately, Mr. President, he is correct about you not getting much done, pertaining to your agenda. The Republicans aren't going to budge unless the VP does. And with the American people wanting to see progress, this could very well fall back on you. Your numbers could slip and when the next election comes around, you could be out of here."

"I'm focusing on the midterms. If the Democrats take back the House and Senate, I'm good. We're going to tackle every item on my agenda and be done with it. After that, the American people can decide whatever. Four years may be enough for me, who knows? In the meantime, I'll be hitting the campaign trail with as many Democrats and Independents as I can. Just make sure they have excellent credentials and don't have me putting myself out there for lazy politicians who are afraid to do anything."

"Never," Andrew said. "I'll be sure to screen everyone and we'll know their real intentions before we visit their hometowns. I've already checked out Florence Green. She's good to go. Her constituents are fired up about her bid for the Senate and they're thrilled about you attending the rally tonight."

"I'm excited and ready to hit the campaign trail again. I need to take care of a few things before we leave, but make sure the governor is there tonight too. I've heard good things about him. Can't wait to meet him."

"He'll be there," Andrew said. "Go ahead and take care of what you need to. We'll see you shortly."

He and Sam left the Oval Office. I hadn't heard from Raynetta all day, so I called her cellphone to check on her.

"Yes," she said.

"Where are you?"

"I'm in my office. Emme and I are going over my schedule. Did you need something?"

"Not really. Just wanted to let you know I'm heading to Virginia this evening for a rally. Probably won't get back until late."

"Okay. Thanks for letting me know. Enjoy yourself."

"I'll try."

We ended the call. Minutes later, I went to the kitchen and asked the chef to put some of Raynetta's favorite oatmeal cookies in a bag. I also asked for a glass of milk. With both items in my hand, I made my way to her office and knocked on the door before entering. She and Emme's heads snapped up. Emme smiled, Raynetta didn't. She closed a binder that was on her desk and laid her pen down.

"Emme, do you mind leaving us alone?" Raynetta said, removing her reading glasses. "We'll resume in about fifteen minutes."

"No problem," Emme said. "I'll go get me a bite to eat and be back soon."

Being very polite as always, Emme spoke to me and left. I put the bag of cookies and milk on Raynetta's desk.

"I thought you could probably use a little snack or something," I said. "Have you eaten anything?"

"I had a salad earlier, but that's it. Thanks for the cookies and milk though."

Even though she had thanked me, I sensed my nice gesture wasn't really appreciated.

"Well, I'll let you get back to work. Enjoy the cookies and I'll see you later."

"I'm sure I will enjoy the cookies, but you don't have to do this, Stephen. I don't want any special treatment from you, okay? Seems like you've been going out of your way to be extra nice. While I appreciate it, I just don't want to get used to it because I know how you are. Besides, you're only doing these things because I'm pregnant."

Trying to avoid an argument, I ignored much of what she'd said and snapped my finger.

"That's right. You are pregnant, aren't you? I almost forgot. How far along are you and when is your next appointment? I would really like to go with you."

"I'm sure you would, but I think I can handle my appointments all by myself."

"I'm sure you can handle them too, but if you don't mind, I'd like to go to your next one with you. Let me know when it is so I can add it to my schedule."

Raynetta displayed a fake grin. "It's tomorrow. Tomorrow at one. If you can't make it, I truly understand."

"Oh, I'll make it for sure. Just don't leave me and don't eat up all of those cookies. I know how much you love them, but too many of those aren't good for you."

"Yeah, I know, so don't keep bringing them to me. Keep the cards too and the milk is a bit much. I don't even like milk."

"I know, but I thought you needed a little something to wash down those cookies. Next time, I'll choose orange juice."

Raynetta playfully rolled her eyes. I made my way to the door and laughed at her reply.

"Apple juice. I hate orange juice too."

Without replying, I smiled and left her office. Several hours later I was in Virginia, exiting Air Force One with my steel gray suit on and white shirt. My waves were flowing and my face was clean shaven. The presidential motorcade awaited me and four black Suburbans were parked around it. Several congressmen and women greeted me. So did numerous Americans who held up signs from afar, cheering for me. Overall, the response was good.

"Thank you for coming this evening," Governor Brown said as he shook my hand. "We are so thrilled about you being here."

He introduced me to several of his staff members and I also met Florence Green who I was rallying for tonight. She was a young African American woman with much enthusiasm. After conversing with her for less than five minutes, I could already tell she would be an asset to the Senate.

"I'm ready," she said after we got inside of the motorcade. "I've been on this journey since I was nineteen years old and now I'm ready to put in the real work."

Her energy and personality made me hyped. And by the time I arrived at the rally, I was prepared to go all in for her. From a distance, I watched her energize the crowd. Her smile alone was warm and inviting. She was also very attractive; I wasn't the only one who thought so. Many of the men in the audience had lust in their eyes, and some flirted with her. She smiled, waved and finally took a seat. Minutes later, I was introduced. The crowd roared, plenty of signs waved in the air and all I could see was a sea of people with T-shirts on that had my image on them. Feeling proud, I stepped to the podium, and after ten long minutes of applause, I started to speak in support of Florence Green. The people of Virginia referred to her as Flo, and every time I said something plausible, they cheered, "Go, Flo, go!" I cheered with them, and with full support for her on display, she couldn't stop smiling. She blew kisses at the crowd, also at me.

"Thank you," she said. "Thank you all and be sure to take all of this energy with you to the voting booth. This is the first step. Come November, I want to be on my way to the Senate!"

More cheers erupted. I finished my fiery speech then stayed a while longer to shake hands.

"Great job, Mr. President," one man said. "We like what you're doing for the American people and we like your style."

"You're the best!"

"Please sign this for me!"

"When will the first lady's next book drop?"

"What hotel are you staying at? I would love to be one of your interns?"

It wasn't long before Secret Service led me away. But instead of heading back to Washington, I was invited to a private fundraising dinner with several congressmen and women. The dinner was $20,000 a plate. Many lobbyists were there, along with wealthy business owners who wanted to make sure their money still had influence. I spoke to some, but kept my distance. Florence also attended, as well as Andrew. He sat next to me at the head table while we listened to Florence speak from another table.

"She's going to win," Andrew whispered to me. "The people of Virginia love her."

"I can tell. What's her story, though? Give me some background on her."

"High school class valedictorian, graduated Magna Cum Laude from Tuskegee University with a degree in political science, no children, father never in the picture, mother is a prominent school teacher and Flo's political views are in line with yours.

There's not much dirt on her, and the only negative press she's gotten is from an ex-boyfriend who claims to have something on her. Many people say he's bitter because she's no longer with him. I say he's a damn fool for letting a woman like her slip through his fingers."

I nodded and we continued to listen to Florence speak.

"The state of Virginia is going to make some real noise in this election," she said. "I can't wait and I want to thank our president for coming all this way to support me. Please stand, Mr. President. We're all so grateful for you, and I look forward to working with you real soon."

I stood and everyone applauded. I didn't want to speak again, so I thanked everyone and sat back down. Minutes later, my food was examined, dinner was served and I spent the evening conversing with many people in the room. The whole time, I noticed Florence watching me. She waited until I'd left the room with a Secret Service agent so I could return a call to Sam. Before I made the call, Florence interrupted me.

"I don't mean to disturb you, Mr. President, but may I speak to you somewhere in private? Just for a few minutes, if you don't mind."

Secret Service heard her request, so when I stepped away, he didn't seem to mind. Florence and I moved to an area that was near a glass staircase.

"I just wanted to thank you again for coming here today," she said. "I know how busy your schedule is and this truly means the world to me. You carried my state by almost fifteen points in the last election. I just want to make sure my constituents know I have your full support."

"No problem and yes you do. I expect to be on the campaign trail a lot this year. And it is my pleasure to get behind candidates like you who I believe in."

She blushed, touched her chest and smiled. "That's awesome. And if you're ever looking for someone to travel with you, don't hesitate to reach out to me. Here is my direct contact information. I sincerely hope this is the beginning of a long-lasting friendship."

She reached out to give me her business card; I took it. I knew what kind of long-lasting friendship she was referring to, but I didn't elaborate on it. Since I hadn't responded, she turned and swished her hips while walking in front of me. Of course I examined her curves from behind—impressive. She interrupted my thoughts when she quickly pivoted and caused me to bump into her. On purpose, her breasts touched my chest before she backed up.

"Sorry about that," she grinned. "I meant to ask if you were traveling back to Washington tonight. If not, I would really like to know where you'll be. Maybe we can celebrate my victory early."

"I'm heading back to Washington tonight, but don't go celebrating too soon. Anything can happen between now and when people go to the polls."

"Anything like what? This?"

Catching me off guard, she leaned in close to me. Her soft lips touched mine, and yet again, her breasts touched my chest. Unlike with VP Bass, this time I was flattered. Even though her actions were aggressive, I didn't necessarily trip. I just backed away and rejected her move.

"I don't think this is a good idea, and there's no need for you to put yourself out there like this. It seems like you're on the right path politically. The last thing you want to do is find yourself in a scandal which can permanently hurt your career. Let's both pretend this conversation never took place. Are you willing to do that?"

She seemed surprised by my response. I guess with all that she'd heard or read about me, she thought this would be easy.

"If you say so," she said. "I'm willing to do whatever, so be sure to keep my personal information close."

She turned again and made her way back into the dining room. I returned Sam's call, but left a message because he didn't answer. When I returned to the dining room, I sat next to Andrew and picked up a glass of water.

"Just so you know," I said to him. "She's going to lose. I have five-hundred bucks on it, and the next time you invite me to speak on someone's behalf, I want you to conduct a more thorough background check. Her ex-boyfriend might be bitter, but whatever dirt he has on her will end her career."

Andrew didn't believe me. However, the very next day the shit hit the fan. Florence's ex released a sex-tape of her in bed with two men. He also released a photo of her kissing me. It was a good thing I hadn't indulged. And even though the photo didn't show me reciprocating, I still had some explaining to do. So did Florence Green. The media wasn't kind to her and they kept showing the salacious video over and over again. It was blurred, but it wasn't a good look. By the end of the day, she was forced to step aside.

First Lady,
Raynetta Jefferson

Stephen was right there for my doctor's appointment, but before the doctor came in, we discussed a photo of him and Florence Green that had been plastered on the news all morning. At first, I didn't know what to make of it. But I was glad Stephen had told me what actually occurred.

"I just don't know what to say about some women," I said while sitting on the examination table. "What kind of Voodoo are you putting on them? Do they not even care you're married?"

"You have no one to blame but yourself. The book you wrote got more women fantasizing about me. I'm sure she read it and thought I would be on board with whatever. As for the Voodoo thing, it's the same kind of Voodoo I put on you many years ago. You couldn't get enough of me, remember?"

I threw my hand back at him and started to nibble at my nail. I was nervous about this appointment; the one I'd had earlier this week consisted of many tests. Stephen didn't go with me because I didn't tell him about my visits. I didn't want him to get too happy about this, because I was still unsure about how to proceed with this. He stood with both hands in his pockets, facing me.

"Did you get the apple juice I left you this morning?" he asked.

"I did and thanks, again, for being so sweet to me. I wonder how long this is going to last?"

"Not long, so don't get used to it."
We both laughed.

"By the way," he said. "Why won't you just have the doctor come to the White House for your visits? It'll be much easier and we won't have to cause a big scene when we come here. The media is already outside waiting for us to leave. They'll be speculating about why we're here. I thought you didn't want anyone to know about the baby just yet."

"Not yet, but maybe soon. I just get tired of being in the White House all the time. Kind of want to have a normal life sometimes. Coming here makes this process feel normal to me."

"I understand that, but what about the delivery? What will you do when our child is delivered? I know you want privacy, don't you?"

I shrugged and hadn't even thought much about it. "I would, but we'll see how it goes."

Stephen took a seat and crossed one leg over the other. By the blank expression on his face, I could tell he didn't approve of my answer. "I think you—"

There was a soft knock on the door so he paused before saying anything else. Dr. Manning came in and greeted both of us. He was a fine, sexy black doctor with mocha chocolate skin, a shiny bald head, a nicely trimmed goatee and a muscle-packed body that was out of this world. I'd been his patient for about two years. He gave good advice too, so I knew he would steer me in the right direction when it came to this baby.

He looked at me, then at Stephen. "Wow. I'm surprised to see you here with Raynetta. Every time she comes, she says you're too busy to come."

His words didn't come across the right way to Stephen. He snapped back.

"Raynetta is a grown woman who doesn't need me to hold her hand at every appointment. And as your president, I am a very busy man. Much busier than you are, *doctor*. When it comes to her appointments relating to our baby, I plan to make time to be here. Hopefully, that satisfies you and her."

Dr. Manning stood with a sly grin on his face. "I wasn't trying to insinuate anything and no offense, Mr. Jefferson."

"Mr. President or President Jefferson is what I prefer. Just as you would like for me to address you as Dr. Manning, instead of a damn fool."

"Call me whatever, but I don't have time to stroke your ego today. I'd like to tell Raynetta about her tests. Unfortunately, I don't have good news to share."

My face twisted and as I looked at Stephen his forehead was lined with wrinkles. I wrapped my arms around my stomach, afraid of what Dr. Manning was going to say. I asked him to clarify his statement.

"What's wrong with me? Please don't tell me—" I swallowed hard as he moved closer to me and placed his hand on my leg to comfort me. A bit of sadness was in his eyes.

"It's the baby, Raynetta. You have what is known as an incompetent cervix. You won't be able to carry your baby full term. By the second trimester you're going to miscarry."

My eyes shifted to Stephen who sat in silence just staring at me. I was so sure he would say something, but so far he hadn't. I looked back at Doctor Manning.

"So, is there anything I can do to save the baby? I mean, what causes this to happen?"

"Many women have this issue and it's rather normal. You can take steps to prevent it from happening again, but pertaining to this pregnancy, there's not much I can do. We need to discuss the best way to end it. No matter what process you decide, there will be side effects like vomiting, nausea, fever chills, blood clotting, diarrhea and a few other complications. But after a few weeks, you should be okay. If you need counseling during this process, I'll be more than happy to recommend someone."

"That won't be necessary, Dr. Manning, but thank you. And if you don't mind, I would like to speak to my husband in private about this."

Comforting me again, he reached out to give me a hug. I appreciated him during this difficult time, because Stephen just sat there like a bump on a log.

"No problem, Raynetta," Dr. Manning released his embrace. "Again, I'm sorry and I wish I had better news."

Without saying a word to Stephen, Dr. Manning walked out. Stephen shot me a perplexed look.

"Why are you looking at me like that? Say something, Stephen. Anything."

"There's not much to say. You got what you wanted. If I wasn't here, you'd be jumping for joy and celebrating with Dr. Manning."

"That's not true so don't even go there. A huge part of me was looking forward to having our baby, but I'm not going to lie and say I wasn't nervous about being a mother. Plenty of women have concerns about that, so please don't go making me feel bad about it."

He stood and moved closer to the examination table. "I don't want you to feel bad about anything, but I was really hoping this worked out. We've been having a lot of bad luck, and every time we take two steps forward, we get pushed five steps back. I wonder why we just can't get ahead. It's frustrating as hell."

"I know exactly how you feel, but in the meantime, I have an important decision to make. Any suggestions?"

Stephen lowered his head and didn't even look at me. "You already know what the doctor recommended. Take his advice and do what you have to do. I'll see you back at the White House."

With sadness on display, he left the room. A kiss or hug would've been nice, but I guess he wasn't feeling it. When Doctor Manning returned, we discussed my options, as well as his confrontation with Stephen.

"I apologize for being so blunt, but the president was out of line."

"That's just how he is. He doesn't bite his tongue and I regret the two of you got off on the wrong foot."

"It didn't surprise me, but I'm sorry this has happened to you. I wish I had better news. Don't give up because an incompetent cervix doesn't prohibit you from having children in the future. As soon as this is over, I suggest you and the president swing back into action and get started again right away. I'm sure he wants to expand his family. What man in his position wouldn't want to?"

"He does, but the problem is me. As you know, I've been bitter about a lot of things. I'm not sure how to move forward with this. Maybe you can help me decide the best way forward."

Dr. Manning stroked his chin and seemed to be in deep thought. "I have some suggestions, but first, Raynetta, you need to put closure to your situation with the baby. If not, you can be anywhere and a miscarriage can happen."

I agreed. And by the end of the day, the pregnancy was over.

President of the United States, Stephen C. Jefferson

There were many ups and downs, and for the next several weeks, I just had to roll with whatever came my way. Deep inside, I was very disappointed about Raynetta's situation. I'd started to get excited about the baby and had hoped for a healthy child soon. But things didn't always go according to my plans. Nothing actually did—this was just me expressing my lack of optimism that hit me during times like this. I spoke to Andrew about it while sitting in his office in the West Wing. We had a big day planned, and for the past few weeks the media had been speculating about what we'd been up to.

"I know things have been rough," Andrew said, leaning back in his chair. His glasses rested on the tip of his nose as he peered over them to look at me. "And I'm sorry to hear about the baby. My wife and I struggled with more of the same thing, so I can relate. After many failed attempts to have a child, we just decided to love each other and get on with our lives without children. It was hard for both of us to do, but when no other options are on the table, what else can you do?"

"I don't think we're to that point yet, but we'll see. Raynetta is slowly but surely getting back to her normal self, but when I try to discuss our next move with a baby, she seems reluctant to talk about it."

"Give her time. These things are very hard on a woman, not to mention what it does to her body. Continue to be there for her. The two of you will be just fine."

"Maybe so. It's hard to have faith in a woman I don't trust and I haven't done so in a very long time. She doesn't trust me either and that's why we continuously have the problems we do."

"What is it about her you don't trust? Has she been with other men?"

"One other man for sure, but my lack of trust revolves around her sneaky ways. She always seems to be up to something and will lie about anything. I've caught her in so many lies. I wouldn't have believed she was pregnant, had I not been there when the nurse confirmed it. I know what I'm saying is bad, but I'm sure you don't feel like you have to watch your back when it comes to your wife."

Andrew stood and buttoned his suit jacket. "I do have to watch my back and so do you. In our positions, there are very little people we can trust. That's just how it has to be, and whether you agree or not, Mr. President, you're hated by many people around the world. It comes with the job, and there are always people plotting to hurt you."

"Based on my Intel briefings, how can I disagree? I have power and problems. Many problems, but it comes with the territory."

Andrew patted my back and smiled. "At least you know. Now, we need to get the ball rolling today. I think I'm more excited about this news than you are."

"I wouldn't say all that, but I'm glad you approve of this. The Republicans may think they can shut me down for the year, but they are sadly mistaken."

We left the West Wing and headed to the Press Briefing Room where Sam was already speaking to the media. I watched him while standing by the door; he had come a long way since day one.

"Rebecca, your assumptions are incorrect," he said to a conservative reporter who often challenged him on every single issue. "I'm not going to continue to break down everything for you. If you need more information on the subject, I suggest you go read a book."

"You mean read a book like the one the first lady wrote? I've already read that one and it leaves me with more questions about the man we have running our country."

"A damn good man," Sam fired back in my defense, before calling on another reporter.

His briefing was quite impressive and when he was done, he stepped aside and allowed me to address the media. I stood behind the podium and cleared my throat. I thought about Michelle as I looked at her empty seat. She would've been proud of me today. All eyes were on me; no one other than Sam and Andrew knew what I was about to say. I started with the facts.

"Despite the many efforts black people have put forth to improve their lives, the wealth disparity between blacks and whites continue to widen. Inequality has plagued African Americans for many years and study after study shows that the black household median wealth is approximately $18,000. Compared to the white household median wealth, which is approximately $170,000, those numbers are staggering. America, we've got to do better than this. Something is very wrong with that picture and how can any of us sit back and think this is okay? If not addressed, blacks, as well as Hispanics, will find themselves completely broke and with nowhere to turn. If you think crime is bad now, just wait and see. In addition to Jim Crow, blacks continue to face other forms of discrimination through our banking institutions, our judicial systems, and I must talk about student loan debt that prohibits too many people from becoming homeowners. The whole system can be summarized as fucked up, and I can go on and on about this, but talk is cheap. As your president, I can no longer sit on my ass in the Oval Office and do nothing. One of the first things I'm going to do is sign an executive order that deals with reparations for slavery. Many have said that doing so would bankrupt our country. My response to that is bullshit. We've waited long enough for those 40 acres and a mule and our day has finally arrived. My administration has discovered ways to pay a lump sum or monthly restitutions to millions of Americans who qualify. We have identified many acres of land, in each state, that can be utilized for business building projects or simply building homes. There will be people within your state who can help you through this process, so I want each and every one of you who qualify to take advantage of what is being offered to you. We're in the business of closing the wealth gap, even though it may take us years and years to do it. But we will, especially for future generations to come. I know that many Americans won't be on board with our plans. Some will challenge me on this and I expect numerous lawsuits to be filed soon. Say what you wish, but don't waste too much time on this. It's going to happen and the action starts today."

I explained more details about my plan, and by the end of my press conference, many reporters sat stone-faced. They appeared to be in total disbelief and you'd better believe there were many questions. One hand after another waved in the air.

"Before I take any questions," I said. "I want all of you to thoroughly read the specifics of my plan. Study it, get a clear understanding of it and then we'll talk again. Until then, have a good day everyone and God bless."

I stepped away from the podium, but one *conservative* reporter was so upset that she came after me. Her whole face was red and tears were in her eyes as she spoke to me through gritted teeth.

"You can't do this, Mr. President! You will bankrupt this country, all for nothing! If reparations could've been rewarded, it would have happened many years ago. Blacks have benefited more from this country than anyone! How much longer are we going to have to hear about injustice and freaking racism?"

If she had spewed her ignorance to me many years ago, I would've slapped the shit out of her. But today was a new day. Thankfully, my head was on straight.

"Your ignorance doesn't deserve a response, but I will offer you one. Get the hell away from me, go educate yourself or suffer the consequences of being an idiot."

She immediately backed away from me with a stunned look washed across her face. Many were stunned, and by four o'clock that evening, death threats were on the rise. Many people were having a fit, including some black people who wanted it to be known they didn't agree. The media welcomed their opinions and happily gave them a platform.

"I just think we need to work harder for what we want. Reparations won't do anything for us, and if all we're going to do is buy Jordans with the money, what good will that do?"

"As a black person, we need to stop taking handouts and look out for ourselves. I disagree with what the president is doing and I won't be applying for any kind of reparations."

"Slavery is over. Let it rest and let's move on. This country has enough problems already. What the president did today was divide us even more."

I sat shaking my head while Andrew and Sam watched the news with me. Sometimes, we were our own worst enemies. I was disappointed by so many blacks being brainwashed; they always wanted to prove racism was a thing of the past.

"I don't get it, Mr. President," Sam said. "While I do believe most Americans agree with you on this, why would any African American speak like this? Do they not know and understand how unfair things are in this country?"

"They get it, but many people are so mentally destroyed and exhausted by what has happened they prefer to ignore it. It's easier that way and whenever someone talks about taking action, it feels better to run away from it. Some people don't want white folks mad at them, and then there are those who truly believe racism no longer exists. I'm just trying to help people who are willing to accept the help. We're going to put them on a path to prosper in the years to come. I can promise you there will be a major change."

"I think so too," Andrew said. "Let's get to our next meeting, which shouldn't last long. The Secretary of Education wants to share some ideas with you."

We all left the Oval Office and headed to the Roosevelt Room for the meeting. On the way there, I saw Raynetta coming my way with a smirk on her face. She had on a tan oversized dress with a belt wrapped around it. Her shoes were flat and her hair was in a ponytail. Without a drop of makeup on, she approached me.

"Are you busy?" she asked. I could smell a hint of alcohol on her breath.

"Yes. I'm on my way to a meeting."

"Well, come here for a second. This shouldn't take that long."

Sam and Andrew looked confused. I asked them to give me a minute, before I stepped into a smaller conference room with Raynetta.

"What's up?" I asked. "And why have you been drinking?"

She sat on the table and pulled at my tie so I could move closer to her. "I had a teeny-tiny drink and that's it. I promise you it's nothing you should worry about, but I was eager to see you so I could do this."

She aggressively covered my mouth with hers and forced her tongue close to my throat. I welcomed her kiss, but I had no idea what this was about.

"Can . . . Can you tell me what's up with this?" I asked then wiped across my wet lips.

She removed the belt from her dress and let it fall open. Her nakedness was now on display.

"I want you to make love to me. Just like you did the last time we were together. If you need to make it quick, I totally understand."

"Are you serious, Raynetta? You know I don't have time for this right now. Let's talk about it later."

She responded with another kiss and another one. And after she reached her hand into my slacks and started massaging my package, my meeting had to wait. We ripped off each other's clothes and found ourselves grinding hard on the shiny, cherry wood conference table.

"Ahhhh, this feels so good," Raynetta said with her head dropped back. "I'm relieved."

She was more than relieved. Her wetness covered me and it wasn't long before I bent her over the table and dug deep from behind. I moved her hair aside, and bent over to plant several kisses along her spine.

"Why are we doing this right now?" I questioned. "Are you trying to get pregnant again?"

She pushed back and grinded to the same rhythm as me while I held her hips. "Yeeeees," she cried out. "I dooo want to and I'm not going to stop until we get what we want."

I had no more words for her; I definitely didn't want to spoil the mood. We would talk more about it later. For now, this was all good. Raynetta kept a tight grip on my steel and after several more minutes of sexy body slapping, I poured my fluids into her. We tightly embraced—our hearts were beating fast.

"This was all so very worth it, wasn't it?" she asked. "Now you can go to your meeting and enjoy the rest of your day."

"I shouldn't have a problem with that, but no more drinking, okay? Please, no more drinking."

Raynetta didn't agree to it, but I didn't have time to discuss it further. I hurried back into my clothes, kissed her goodbye, tidied up in the bathroom and went into my meeting.

The meeting went on longer than expected. I had to read and sign off on a few documents that were on my desk, and before the day was over, I'd promised my Secretary of Health and Human Services I would get back to him regarding some changes he wanted to make in his department. I was at my desk for hours, before a call was transferred to me from Florence Green.

"Hello, Mr. President," she said. "I guess I should've called you sooner to apologize for the photo, but I've been in damage control over here. I made a decision to step away from the race, but aside from my personal life, I know I'm capable of doing the job. I regret approaching you the way I did, but in my defense, I'm attracted to handsome and intelligent men. Please take that as a compliment, and if there is anything you can help me do or any suggestions you have that can help me repair my reputation, I'd like to hear them."

"I know all about those personal issues, but don't allow anyone to make more noise about those things than they do about your life-long accomplishments. Take one day to discuss your personal issues, be as honest as you can be about it and move on. Politics is a very dirty business. We all have skeletons, but some people just do a better job at hiding theirs than others. I'm not sure how much more I can help you, especially since many people already believe we're involved. Nonetheless, good luck with everything. I'll be following what happens in your state and thanks for reaching out to me."

"Thank you too, Mr. President. Good luck with everything and I appreciate you for taking my call."

We ended the call and I sat for a moment thinking about what an unfortunate situation Florence had gotten herself in. There was no question she could've been an asset to the Senate, but with the baggage she had, it halted her progress in every way. When it pertained to men in politics having affairs, sleeping with prostitutes . . . many Americans were forgiving. The same didn't apply to women—they were required to throw in the towel right away. Their reputations were ruined and many never recovered. It wasn't fair, but that's how politics operated. I hadn't had an opportunity to check out the full sex video with Flo in it, so just for the hell of it I picked up my phone to watch. Nearly five minutes in, I was shocked. Her head game was fierce, and while tackling two men at once, it really wasn't a good look. I stopped the video and thought about her political future. In my opinion, it was a wrap.

Thirty minutes later, I went to the Executive Residence to call it a night. As I entered the Master Suite, Raynetta surprised me again. This time, she was completely naked. Her hair was still in a ponytail and her legs were tightened around a body pillow.

"You're right on time," she said. "I was almost on my way to come get you from the Oval Office."

I sat on the bed next to her and removed my tie. "Listen to me, okay? I know you're still trying to cope with what happened, but the last thing we both need is for you to start drinking. It's only going to make matter worse, Raynetta, and it's not going to solve one single problem."

"I know it won't." She removed my suit jacket and started to unbutton my shirt. "I told you I would keep my drinking under control and the only reason I've been doing it is to numb some of my pain. There's so much pain and I don't know if you understand how deep it is."

"Maybe I don't, but tell me about your pain. Are you still bitter or does this have more to do about the baby?"
She shrugged and displayed a grin. "This is pain that I'll work through and eventually get over."
"Let me help you then. Tell me what else I can do."
Without replying, Raynetta pulled me closer to her. I removed my clothes and lay between her soft legs. I rubbed them as she secured them around my waist and gazed into my eyes.

"Help me how?" she whispered. "Are you going to help me overcome this?"

"Yes, I will. I will help to take away your pain, but you have to put in some work too. Okay?"

She nodded and reached down to direct my steel inside of her. At first, the pace was smooth and deliberate. But when she straddled herself on top to ride me, she was moving so fast I couldn't keep up. Every time she slammed down on me, my back lifted from the bed. My hands kept slipping from her sweaty backside and my heart was beating fast.

"Wa . . . Wait a minute, baby," I grunted. "Slow down and take your time with this. I'm right here and I'm not going anywhere."

She slowed her pace and just as I felt her folds tighten, I positioned her over my face to cool down her insides. Unfortunately, it was a bad move on my part. She hammered my lips, and her speedy movements caused my neck to jerk around. The good thing was the sweet taste of her fluids. Bad thing was my neck was in a lot of pain. Even more pain when she forced me back and had my whole head hanging off the bed. I was trying to keep my balance while satisfying her at the same time.

"You . . . You are alleviating my paaaaain!" she shouted during an orgasm. "I luuuuv how you make me feel!"

I was glad to hear that, but later that night I couldn't even sleep. My neck was so sore that I had to take two aspirins to ease my pain. Raynetta was sound asleep. I'd thought she'd had enough, but as I tackled the golf course the next day with four members of the Congressional Black Caucus, she interrupted us. Since she had on a white skirt, polo shirt and a visor, they assumed she was there to join us. That was the furthest thing from her mind. What was on her mind became obvious when she pulled me into a waiting area where many golf carts were. She started kissing me and telling me how much she needed me.

"I know you do," I said as she stood in front of me. "But we can't keep doing this while I'm in the middle of doing things."

"Says who?" she asked and lifted her skirt. She removed her panties and tucked them into my pocket. "You can do whatever you want and whenever you want to do it."

She secured her arms around my sore neck and pushed herself up on the tips of her toes. To relieve the pressure from my neck, I lifted her to my midsection. She straddled her legs around me, and yet again, one thing led to another. Our spontaneous sex sessions went on for multiple weeks. I was exhausted and I couldn't help but to think Raynetta was up to something, other than getting pregnant again.

First Lady,
Raynetta Jefferson

From my point of view, I had been feeling a little better. But even on my good days, I couldn't forget certain things. Stephen had been there for me more than he'd been in a long time. That not only consisted of sex, but it was a combination of sending me "thinking of you" cards, calling to see how I was doing, having some of my favorite dishes cooked for me and today he'd sent me some flowers. I appreciated the slight change in him, but I kind of felt like he was doing nice things so I wouldn't be so reluctant about the baby. I had definitely been trying to get pregnant again, and after my unfortunate circumstances, I realized how foolish it was not to trust myself as a mother. I would be a wonderful mother and there was no question in my mind Stephen would be an excellent father. Certain things about my past caused me to think otherwise about bringing a child into this world, and with having a screwed up childhood, I feared for my child as well. There were some cruel people out there who took advantage of children. I would be so overprotective of our child and I would never let the same thing happen to our child, like they'd happened to me and Stephen. With me being molested and Stephen living such a rough life, it messed us up. Maybe he'd gotten completely over it, but I had a tendency to hold on to things and keep them bottled up inside. I also held grudges. And revenge, at the highest levels, felt so good to me.

As for drinking, I had to admit I'd been drinking too much. It started off with just one drink here and there, but just this morning I found myself needing something stronger than coffee. I had a long day ahead of me at a ceremony where I was being honored for my contributions and dedication to improving education in the inner cities. The function started at noon; I was already running late. Stephen was on the campaign trail again. He'd left this morning to hold another rally, and after another energetic night in the bedroom, I was feeling pretty good. I'd gone to Dr. Manning to let him run some more tests. The pregnancy test I'd taken showed negative, and when I called him, he still didn't have any news I wanted to hear.

"No, Raynetta, you're not pregnant yet. I know you and the president are trying really hard, but sometimes these things take time. Keep taking your meds and give it more time. It's bound to happen again and when it does everything will be set."

I wanted to believe him, but something in my gut told me my outcome would be different.

"Thank you," I said. "I'm definitely doing my part over here and I'm following the doctor's orders."

He laughed and told me he had to take another call. Right after my call ended with him, my phone rang. It was my agent. I'd been ignoring her phone calls because I didn't want to argue with her about not turning in another book.

"I wish you would stop calling me so much," I barked. "Don't you have anything else to do with your time?"

"I certainly do, Raynetta, but you can't go around breaking contracts. The publisher is going to sue you. You'll be getting a letter soon. You'll have thirty days to turn in something. I suggest you consider a ghostwriter, but that's totally up to you. Let me know what you decide and please give this more thought."

"I will, but I'm not sure if I'll change my mind. Goodbye and please wait until I call you."

I hit the end button on my phone and dropped it in my purse. After I tossed back another glass of alcohol, I headed for the door. At first, the alcohol didn't seem to affect me. But right as I was at the ceremony, about to accept my award, I started to feel woozy. The room was hot and it started to spin. All I could hear was laughter and a bunch of applause.

"Go," Emme said, shoving me towards the podium. "Go get your award. They're waiting on you."

I widened my eyes and took several steps forward. My legs felt weak, and by the time I reached the podium, I had to hold on to it in order to stay standing. The crowd appeared real fuzzy and the bright lights made me squint. With so many eyes locked on me, I became nervous.

"Tha . . . Thank you all for thisss," I slurred and hiccupped. "I'm glaaad that my contributions helped and I will continue to do more."

There was light applause. And when the crystal award was given to me, I couldn't even hold it. It was too heavy; it slipped from my hands and crashed when it hit to the floor. Shards flew everywhere and loud gasps escaped in the room. Emme and a Secret Service agent rushed on stage to get me. They escorted me away as I covered my mouth in shame.

"Did I do good?" I asked Emme. "I did, didn't I?"

Emme nodded and held my hand with hers. "You did. But you're capable of doing so much better than this."

The ride back to the White House was quiet. By then, I started to realize the damage I had done. Nearly everyone at the White House looked strangely at me. Some asked if I was okay.

"I'm fine," I said, before making my way to the Executive Residence. Emme helped me up the stairs. She even ran bath water for me, after I had asked. I sat on the edge of the bed, while removing my shoes and watching the breaking news.

"What is wrong with her?" A reporter asked. "Was she intoxicated or is she on drugs?"

"I've seen that look before," another reporter said. "She's on drugs, probably heroin or cocaine. Either way, this is bad."

"It is bad. I've never seen or heard of a first lady conduct herself in this manner."

I threw my shoe at the TV. "Well, go to the National First Ladies Library and read about it, you idiot! Some were worse than me and what about the numerous ones who had affairs, had lesbian relationships, refused to sleep in the same bed as their husbands, stole money, were addicted to pain medication and were alcoholics? And one wasn't even the president's wife! She was his niece! Did you forget about that?"

"Come on in the bathroom," Emme said, pulling me away from the TV. "Don't look at that garbage. Your bath water is ready. I hope the temperature isn't too hot for you."

I sluggishly made my way to the bathroom. "Thanks, Emme. Close the bedroom door on your way out and turn off the TV. I don't want to hear any more negative things said about me."

Emme left the bathroom and followed my orders. After I stripped naked, I sunk my body in the Jacuzzi tub with lots of bubbles. I rested my head back on the contoured pillow and closed my eyes. I couldn't even explain how a few swigs of alcohol had snuck up on me, and more than anything, I was embarrassed. I knew this wouldn't go over well with Stephen, and after less than fifteen minutes in the tub, he appeared in the doorway. His hands were in his pockets, eyes were contracted as he looked my way.

"Tell me this," he said. "Why do you keep doing this to us, Raynetta? Why do you keep fucking up and what is it inside of you that keeps you on a destructive path?"

His voice was calm, so mine remained calm too. "I had one drink earlier. By the time I got to the ceremony, something triggered my whole body. I became dizzy and couldn't even walk or talk. I know it looked bad, but it's not as bad as it seems."

Stephen came further into the bathroom and stood by the tub. He touched the side of my face and lifted my chin so I could look at him.

"You're not going to do this to us. I won't let you, Raynetta, and if you need help, you'd better go get it."

I smacked his hand away from my face. "I told you I was fine, didn't I? Stop trying to make this about more than what it is, and I know exactly what you're thinking about. You're thinking about the situation with your mother. I guess if I don't get my act together, I'm going to wound up like her too."

"That's exactly what I'm afraid of, and if you keep standing in the way of my peace and happiness, the rules do apply. You can lie to me all you want, but one drink my ass. I have enough bullshit to explain to the American people. I don't have time to go out there and clean up your mess too."

His pitch was higher. Knowing I was wrong, I attempted to cool things down.

"You don't have to explain anything for me. I'll explain and I promise you that it's not as serious as you think."

He left the bathroom and came back with my large leather purse in his hand. "Not that serious, huh? How many bottles of alcohol are in here?"

Without answering, I stood and reached for a towel to wrap myself with it.

"How many, Raynetta?" he yelled.

"None." I walked up to him. "Now calm down and give me my purse."

He wouldn't give it to me. He stepped away from me and placed my purse on the counter. As he rambled through it, I tried to snatch it but he pushed me away.

"One," he said and slammed the small bottle of Vodka on the counter. "Two! Three! Three fucking bottles of alcohol and you want to tell me it's not that fucking serious!"

He picked up one of the bottles and smacked it against the counter. Glass flew everywhere; one piece sliced his hand. "I'm not doing this with you!" he yelled. "Do you fucking hear me, Raynetta! I will hurt you for this shit and have no regrets!"

My whole body shook. I felt horrible about this, and as I looked at the deep cut on his hand, I stepped forward to help him. He snatched his hand away from me and pushed me back again.

"Go get you some help, please!"

I didn't respond. It was already a messed up situation and I didn't want to say the wrong thing. I moved forward again; this time I wrapped my arms around him and attempted to kiss him. He turned his head and backed away from me.

"No. We're not going there again. I'm tired of fucking. My neck hurts, my dick hurts and so does my head. My hand too, so get away from me, Raynetta. Go chill or call the doctor so he can assist you with whatever it is you're still dealing with."

He turned on the faucet and ran water over his bloody hand. I stood behind him and started to explain *some* of my issues.

"I just want to get pregnant again. I'm feeling like I let you down and when I called Dr. Manning today he said nothing has changed."

"So what, Raynetta. If we're given another opportunity to have a child, great. If not, we just have to love ourselves, appreciate our lives, be thankful for what we have and go on from there."

"But you looked so disappointed the day of my doctor's appointment. Like you hated me or something. I felt like a failure. That's why I've been trying so hard to make this right."

He wrapped his hand with a towel then turned to face me. "You're not a failure and trust me when I say I'm okay with what has happened. We don't always get everything in life we want, nobody does. Now what else is troubling you? Get it all out and let's be done with this."

"My book deal. The publishing house wants to sue me, because I don't want to submit another book. I can't even think straight right now and the last thing I want to do is cause more separation between us."

"In my spare time, I'll write it. Who else can tell the rest of the story better than me? Now that that problem is solved, what else?"

"I'm so embarrassed by what I did today. How can I explain this to the American people?"

"I'll do it. Just be sure to call the doctor and set up an appointment to see someone who can help you work through this."

"I will. I promise you I will and thank you for everything." I dropped the towel and smiled at him. "Meanwhile, will you help me with this?"

He moved his head from side-to-side while keeping the direction of his eyes above my chin.
"I don't know what kind of pills you're taking, but you have been on a roll. I can't help you today because I have to go calm this situation with you, before things get too out of control. I also missed my Intel briefing earlier, so I need to get caught up to speed. Just so you know, there is a limit to how much sex I can have. I wasn't joking when I told you how sore my body is. I guess I'm getting too old."

"Tell that to someone who isn't on the receiving end of your love making skills. You got it going on, Mr. President, and I can vouch for you any day, all day."

Stephen seemed calmer, and right after he left to go back to work, I started to clean up. I threw the broken glass in the trash, along with one of the other bottles of alcohol. The other bottle remained in my hand. I pondered for a while, before putting it back into my purse. I was sure to get rid of it later.

President of the United States, Stephen C. Jefferson

Two days after the incident with Raynetta, we sat down for an interview that was long overdue. We had an opportunity to explain multiple things being discussed around the country, and the interviewer, Mr. Coleman, hit us with numerous questions regarding our personal lives. Some of it was answered, some I prompted him to move on. When it came to Raynetta explaining what had happened at the ceremony that day, she told me to stay silent while she spoke up.

"My doctor subscribed some pain pills for me that made me real nauseous. And right before the ceremony took place, I had a glass of wine to celebrate my assistant's birthday. The pills and alcohol didn't go well together. What everyone witnessed was the end result. I could barely breathe and I was so weak. Many people thought I was on drugs or highly intoxicated but I wasn't. I take offense to those kinds of things being said about me, but at the end of the day, the people who dislike me will do so regardless. I'm much better now. No more pain pills, and the next time I'll have another glass of wine is when the president and I celebrate our baby. We're finally working on having a little one."

"That's wonderful. I'm sure your mother is happy about the news too, Mr. President. Have you spoken to her since she's been incarcerated? I don't know if the two of you still keep in touch, but if you do, I'm sure she's thrilled about possibly being a grandmother."

Raynetta and I had prepared answers for everything. "My mother is no longer behind bars. She was released and I guess she's somewhere awaiting her trial. I have not spoken to her, but wherever she is I wish her well. What she did was unfortunate, but just like any other citizen in this country, she is not above the law. Ultimately, a jury will have to decide her fate."

"That's a courageous thing to say. I can only imagine how all of this makes you feel, and I hope everything works out for the best. What I'm not so sure about is the executive order you signed a few weeks ago. It's causing quite an uproar around the country and some people aren't real happy about it. Can you share more details about your reparations plan? I've read through the entire plan and I'm still unsure about how this is supposed to work. Who will actually benefit the most from it and who will lose?"

I didn't want to, but I spent the next twenty minutes or so, explaining how everything would work. After I was done, we all shook hands and the interview was over. I returned to the Oval Office. Raynetta left the White House with Emme—by the time they reached their destination, many Americans' views about Raynetta had changed again.

"She's so brave," one reporter said. *"I can't imagine being in her shoes. If you ever want to know the truth about something, all you have to do is ask."*

"That's what I love about the first lady and the president. They always tell it like it is. You can truly sense how much the two of them love each other."

I turned off the TV and leaned back in my chair. Unfortunately, in order for me to keep this country moving forward, sometimes, the lies were necessary. There were certain things no one needed to know, and I wasn't about to sit back and watch people tear Raynetta apart over this. She had, indeed, been through enough.

Later that day, I was on my way to Alabama for another rally. This time, I was speaking on behalf of a thirty-five-year-old young man who had much political potential. His resume was stellar and he could be very valuable to me in the Senate. Even though he was a black man from Alabama, he had a lot of support. I wasn't so sure if it would be enough to fight off his Republican challenger in November, but we were all fighting hard to make sure this country was moving forward, instead of backwards.

My team and I arrived at seven o'clock that evening. The school gymnasium was packed. Numerous speakers had already been at the podium, and as I remained in the back speaking to Shawn Jacobs about his aspirations, he impressed me. Kind of reminded me of myself; therefore, I intended to do everything I could to help him secure a spot in the Senate.

"You've been nothing but an inspiration to me," he said. "One of these days, I hope to be president too. I know it's a lot of work, but nothing comes easy."

"No it doesn't, but let's work on getting you to the Senate first. Are you ready to go out there and make some noise?"

He slapped his hand against mine. "You'd better believe I am. Let's go."

Shawn and I headed to the podium together. The crowd was so loud that my ears were ringing. He stood at the podium first, but the second he opened his mouth, a loud popping sound went off. His whole body jerked back, and right after he fell against me, the popping sound came again. I felt a burning sensation in my left arm. I didn't realize I'd been shot until I saw blood oozing down my shirt and I heard Secret Service yelling over the noise.

"Get down, Mr. President, and stay down!"

"Cover him nowwwww!"

I heard more bullets whizzing through the air, and as one of my agents was on top of me, I heard him grunt.

"I've been hit," he yelled. "Code 7!"

The gunfire had stopped, but there was so much chaos from people trampling over each other to exit and screaming. I didn't have time to see much of anything because six Secret

Service agents rushed me off the stage. I did, however, see two white men on the floor with multiple gunshot wounds.

"The president was shot!" I heard a woman say. "I think he's dead!"

"So is Shawn! Somebody go help him, please!"

It was a mess. I was rushed outside and damn near thrown into a black Suburban with tinted windows. The driver sped away and rushed me to the hospital. A doctor was already inside of the SUV to see about my wound. I lay on the seat, squeezing my eyes while trying to ease the pain. My blood was all over the seat and my whole left arm was starting to feel numb.

"If you can," the doctor said. "Lay flat on your back and relax, Mr. President. We'll be at the hospital in no time, but I need for you to be as still as possible while I do this."

I squeezed my fists together as he added pressure around my wound. He was trying to slowdown the bleeding, but it was oozing fast from my arm. I started to feel lightheaded and I kept opening and closing my eyes. A tingling feeling was taking over my body, and no one was more relieved than me when we arrived at the hospital. I was rushed to a private surgery room, and with numerous bright white lights shining in my face, several doctors worked on me.

I cracked my eyes open and looked at the clock next to me. It was five-after-three in the morning and the room I was in was frigid. Only a white thin sheet covered me, the curtains were closed and there was no TV in the spacious room. The bed I was in was comfortable. A leather reclining chair was next to it and a shelf with numerous books on it was to my right. My whole left arm was wrapped and all I'd had on was a white tank shirt and striped pajama pants. I didn't know how I'd gotten to the room, but there was a wheelchair close by the door. My mind traveled to what had happened. This was my second time being shot—thankfully, I survived. Four other presidents before me were assassinated and all were killed by gunshot wounds. Aside from those presidents, there had been plenty assassination attempts involving bombs and planes that were supposed to fly into the White House. Those plots had been foiled, and after this episode, I considered myself lucky. Secret Service acted fast. Just not fast enough. I didn't know my agent's or Shawn's condition—I wondered who else had been injured. I could see several people outside of the door, but when I tried to sit up, my body was so stiff I could barely move. My arm was still in much pain. An IV was in my hand and my lips were so dry that they stuck together. A pitcher of ice water was next to me, but I couldn't reach it. Thankfully, I didn't have to buzz anyone. Within a few more minutes, two doctors entered the room. So did Raynetta, and Andrew stood close by the door. Before the doctors said anything, Raynetta rushed up to me. The second she leaned in to kiss me, I smelled alcohol on her breath.

"I'm so glad you're okay," she said, blowing her hot breath on me and kissing all over my face. "You have to stop scaring me like this."

I just looked at her and said nothing. She sensed exactly what I was thinking. It wasn't long before she backed away from me and cleared her throat.

"Can I get you anything?" she asked then looked at the doctors. "He may want some water. Please get him some water and some pain pills too."

"Pain pills will be fine," I confirmed. "And a fifth of Gin, if you got it. Better yet, what you can get is the hell out of here, Raynetta. Leave now. I'll deal with you later."

She cocked her head back and shot me a dirty look as if she didn't approve of what I'd said. "Excuse me, but what are you—"

"Andrew, get Secret Service in here. I want her gone. Right now."

"But Mr. President. She's—"

"Mr. President my ass! Do like I politely asked and get her out of here now!"

Secret Service had already entered the room. Raynetta was asked to leave, but she didn't go quietly.

"This makes no sense," she said, snatching away from Secret Service. "And don't either of you touch me. I will leave, but I'll be back soon."

She was escorted out of the room. Everyone who remained was in awe, including the doctors who stood with their mouths dropped open.

"Tell me the damage so I can get out of here," I said. "I guess it couldn't be too bad if I'm still alive."

One of the doctors stepped forward to speak to me. "Yes, it's always a good thing when the president is still alive. We removed the bullet from your arm, but you lost a lot of blood. We're giving you a blood transfusion, and we would like for you to stay, at least, another day because the bullet fractured your bone, shattering it. We had to repair it. Your muscles were torn, so you're going to feel a substantial amount of pain from time to time. We've given you antibiotics and pain medicine already. Drinking plenty of fluids is vital. Your arm is going to be severely sore for a while, but I want you to exercise it as much as you can. If you think you need more pain medicine, please let me know."

My eyes shifted to Andrew who stood with a mean mug on his face. His arms were folded across his chest; he appeared eager to speak to me.

"I'll stay for another day, but I need to speak to my chief of staff in private."

"No problem, Mr. President," the other doctor said. "We'll get your pills and water as the first lady requested. Is there anything else we can get you?"

"Nothing else. Thanks."

After giving me some pain medicine and water, the doctors left the room. Andrew stood at the edge of the bed, shaking his head.

"I don't know how this happened, Mr. President. That place was highly secured and everyone had been checked before entering. The FBI is investigating. There is a chance that the guns those clowns used were placed in the gymnasium several days before you arrived. The men who did the shooting were shot and killed. Agent Saunders is going to be okay, and thank God Shawn is going to be fine too. He got out of surgery a few hours ago."

I felt relieved. There was no question Secret Service had dropped the ball again, but overtime I'd learned how difficult their jobs really were. Protecting the president was no easy task, especially one like me who had received hundreds of death threats. Those threats were never made known to the public, but it was a lot to deal with.

Andrew gave me more insight regarding the racist shooters, and to sum it up, it was the result of angry white men who felt as if my recent actions with reparations would destroy America. I regretted Shawn and my agent had been injured because of me. But I was sure that if Shawn had to do it all over again, he wouldn't have changed one thing.

I was released from the hospital a day later. We did our best to keep my departure low-key, but the second I left the hospital, someone leaked my release and the media was right there. I was rushed to the motorcade and taken to the airport where I boarded Air Force One. Multiple phone calls came in, but Andrew took the calls while I sat back in my chair, closed my eyes and waited anxiously to get home.

"We're almost at the White House, Mr. President," Andrew said. "The press is already to full capacity on the South Lawn. When Marine One lands, just keep moving."

He didn't have to give me directions because I wasn't in the mood for questions. As soon as Air Force One landed, I got on Marine One that arrived at the White House minutes later. The South Lawn was lit up with bright lights, cameras and plenty of folks from the media. I exited Marine One and couldn't move fast enough with Secret Service surrounding me.

"Mr. President, what do you have to say about the men who shot you?"

"Are you concerned about another hit on you, Sir?"

"Do you regret signing that executive order?"

The questions went on and on. I headed inside, stopped by the Oval Office to get a few things and then went to the Executive Residence. Raynetta was in the Master Suite sleeping peacefully in a pair of yellow lace panties and no shirt on. I leaned over her and inhaled. Sure enough, the smell of Vodka hit me. I moved back to a chair that was beside our bed and took a seat. Removed my shirt and laid it across my lap. Kicked my shoes off and relaxed. The only thing I had on were my slacks because I needed somewhere to tuck the rope I'd had. I whistled and tapped my foot on the floor. After I cleared my throat, Raynetta jumped from her sleep and quickly sat up in bed. She rubbed her messy hair back with her hand and squinted as she looked at me in the dim room.

"Stephen, is that you? We . . . When did you get here?"

"Wouldn't you like to know? Then again, you really don't care, Raynetta. And to be honest, neither do I anymore."

She sat up and tried to explain her actions, once again. "After I found out you'd been shot, I was scared. I didn't know what to do and I rushed to the hospital in fear. I had one drink. You act as if I came to the hospital like a drunken fool who couldn't control myself."

I reached for the rope, twirling it in my hands. My head remained down and I spoke in a soft tone.

"Who are you—"

Raynetta quickly cut me off. "I know where you intend to go with this, but how can you threaten me when you know I may possibly have an addiction? Maybe I do, Stephen, but does it make you feel good to come in here like this and try to scare me? If you're going to do anything with that rope, go right ahead. Do what you must, but if I go, so will you."

I lifted my head and watched Raynetta ease her hand from underneath the pillow. She pulled out a gun and placed it on her lap.

"Yes, there are times when I'm afraid of what you will do," she said. "It's not a good feeling to have to sleep with one eye open sometimes. I feel like I have to keep this handy and in no way do I ever take your threats lightly."

"You shouldn't because, many times, I mean what I say. And this time, let's see who really has the balls to follow through."

I stood and made my way up to the bed. I felt my arm throbbing, but it didn't prevent me from holding the rope in my other hand. Raynetta quickly picked up the gun and held it in her hand. I tossed the rope on the bed and lifted her hand so her gun could touch my chest.

"Go ahead and shoot me. Kill me, Raynetta, and finish me off. This is your chance. You keep talking about how much I've done to you, but day by day you're killing me. You're destroying my lifelong dreams, prohibiting me from being all I can be and you're bringing me unnecessary bullshit that is no different from the lifetime of chaos my mother brought me. So let's get this over with, so when I'm gone, you can drink all you want to and find someone else to blame for your problems. You'll no longer have to sleep with one eye open and all of your fears will be gone. You have the power, right now, to settle your problems. In an instant, they'll be over and you can say it was suicide. If you need me to write a note, I'll happily do it."

"Then open the drawer, remove a notebook and pen and start writing it. I'll tell you exactly what you need to say."

With her gun still close to my chest, I inched over to the nightstand and pulled out a notebook and pen. I sat on the bed next to her while she kept the gun on me.

"Tell me what to say. Dear who, what and why?"

"Write Dear Raynetta, the only woman who has loved me, despite all of my flaws. I'm so deeply sorry for the pain I've caused you, and I understand how difficult it must be for you to pick up the pieces from our marriage and carry on. I will continue to help you fight your demons, because when I spent years fighting mine, you never completely turned your back on me. You hung in there with me and your love for me never wavered. I was a fool to fall in love with another woman. I made a mistake and I wholeheartedly apologize for asking you to divorce me. I never should have done that and I know it may take years, not months, to repair the damage I've caused. With all my heart, I love you. That's right, I love you and I will do whatever it takes to prove just how much I do. Sincerely yours, your husband."

I hadn't written one word. The pen tapped the notebook and I finally laid it on the bed next to the gun Raynetta had placed there as well.

"What this all boils down to is me admitting to falling out of love with you and loving another woman. I don't know if you'll ever be able to move on from this, Raynetta, but it is important for me to be as honest as I can with you. I can write your words on paper, but it may take some time for me to feel the way you want me to feel. Right now, I don't, mainly because I don't trust you."

"Why don't you trust me? What have I done to make you not trust me?"

I searched deep into her eyes, hoping she could sense where I was coming from. "You know better than me and there isn't enough time left to keep pretending and lying. You're filling your body with a poison that is going to destroy you. That alcohol is going to take everything from you and the problems we have will continue. I'm begging you not to go down this path and I'm trying to save you. For the sake of saving yourself, not for our marriage, not out of love for me, not because you can't have it your way, please see about you. Can you do that, please?"

She swallowed and didn't appear to take anything I'd said seriously. "I will. This time I will and I'll make an appointment tomorrow."

Raynetta moved away from me and sat against the headboard. She laid a pillow on her lap and patted it.
"Come lay down. I'm so sorry about what happened in Alabama. I talked to Andrew who told me about those idiots. I'm so afraid for you, Stephen. What impresses me the most about you is every time you get knocked down, you get back up and keep roaring back again."

I laid my head on the pillow and looked at her. "The same can be said for you, but I'll also be sleeping with one eye open, especially since I didn't know you had a gun underneath your pillow."

"It's a good thing I had it. I have a feeling if I didn't, you would have choked me to death with that rope."
I refused to confirm. "I'll never tell. Just have to watch my back, always."

"Same here. Hate it has to be this way, but I guess this is what a whole lot of dysfunction feels like, huh?"

"That and then some. I just wonder if we can figure out a way to get rid of the dysfunction."

Raynetta sat silent. My eyes shifted to the gun and rope on the bed. We were both lucky we'd made it through another day without killing each other at 1600 Pennsylvania Ave. There were several presidents and first ladies who couldn't get along while living here, but there was no question we had taken things to a new level.

First Lady,
Raynetta Jefferson

I was sitting in the dining room having lunch. The TV was on and I watched Stephen and Shawn standing in front of a crowd of people who filled the gymnasium. They both had been injured, but were back on the campaign trail again.

"We won't let them put fear in us," Stephen said with his arm in a sling. "They're not going to stop us from moving forward and I will take as many bullets as I have to, in order to handle the people's business!"

The crowd went crazy. They loved every bit of it and Stephen's braveness was courageous to many.

"I don't want you to let anyone silence you either. Speak up at the polls next week, vote for Shawn and show those idiots there aren't enough bullets in this world to stop this movement. We have work to do and that work is going to get done by any means necessary!"

The crowd cheered again. Stephen stepped aside for Shawn to speak. His speech was just as fiery. I smiled and had to give credit where it was due. They made one hell of a team. I downed my apple juice, had another piece of toast, and then headed to Dr. Manning's office so he could give me an update and some direction. He always made time to see me, and when I stepped inside of his office, he hurried to end his call.

"Have a seat, Raynetta. I know you have a lot on your mind and so do I. I'm here to help, as always."

I sat in a chair in front of his desk and crossed my legs. I released a deep sigh and looked at him with worry in my eyes.

"This is too much," I admitted. "My drinking is getting out of control and I don't even want to mention the stress. I'm giving up on trying to have a baby, and I can't really say Stephen wants one either."

"Please don't give up. You've come too far and you're almost there. I want you to talk to a private counselor who can help with your drinking issues. I don't think it's anything serious and you have to know that you've been under a lot of pressure. Rehab is good, but you don't need people in your business. And after you find out you're pregnant, you won't even think about another drink. All you'll have time to think about is the baby and how you're going to spend a very good life with me."

His words made me smile. I couldn't wait to have the good life I deserved. It became apparent, many months ago, I could never have it with Stephen. I would never, ever be able to forgive him for what he'd done. Planning to kill me and falling in love with Michelle was my turning point. I could no longer play the fool, so my plans had to change. As for Teresa, I didn't give a hoot about him killing her. I wanted her to get out of jail and deal with Stephen, so I wouldn't have to. But like always, he was ten steps ahead of everyone. When it came to me, however, he wasn't. At least I didn't think he was, until last night. My gut told me he knew something, but maybe it was just me. I had to pay more attention to his actions—didn't want to get caught slipping. And while I still had love for Stephen, I hated him enough to destroy him, once and for all. Dr. Christopher Manning was going to help me do it.

"I'll tell you what," I said to Chris. "I haven't had this much sex in a long time. Either I'm going to get pregnant by you or Stephen. This baby needs to hurry up before he gets suspicious. I sensed something with him last night, but I'm not sure."

"Well, I've been doing my part and I've enjoyed every minute of it. I do hope that when you get pregnant the baby is his. That way, we'll have a child who will be set for life. If it's a boy, be sure to name him after his father."

"Of course I will. Now, what's our next move?"

"I still want you to speak to a counselor about your drinking issues. You can speak to her about your feelings too. She's good and I'm sure the two of you will become friends. Don't forget to share your initiatives with Stephen. He needs to see some progress and keep on trying to make that baby. Encourage him to get started on those books so we can keep more money in our pockets. And just when he thinks everything is on the right path, we're going to pull the rug from underneath him."

That thought made me smile again. "You know I almost shot him last night. He came into the bedroom, trying to threaten me with a rope. I surprised him with a gun, and it would've been the perfect opportunity for me to say it was self-defense. But I thought about how important it is to have this baby."

"Very important, but if it doesn't happen soon, we'll work around it."

I nodded and expressed my feelings to Chris. "Nobody knows how hard this has been for me. I don't even think you know how difficult it is for me to be around a man who has no love for me."

Chris got up from his desk and squatted in front of me. He held my hands with his and made me feel much better.

"I love you, beautiful. And this will all be over with soon. Just stay the course and go talk to the counselor I'm going to recommend. It will help and all the stress you're feeling will soon be a thing of the past."

He leaned in to hug me, and after a lengthy kiss, I went to the counselor he'd suggested.

I spent nearly two hours with the counselor and left her office on a high note. I had gone all evening without a drink and had thrown away the bottle of Vodka that was in my purse. My main focus now was getting pregnant. Stephen had been sleeping in the Master Suite more often, but at three in the morning he wasn't there. I got out of bed to go look for him. Sometimes, he'd slept on the Truman Balcony, others times I could find him in the

Yellow Room or in the Oval Office. Tonight I found him wide awake on the Truman Balcony, writing. A sheet was wrapped around me as I stepped up to him and sat on his lap.

"What are you writing? It's a little chilly out here. I thought you'd be in bed by now."

"I'm not tired. Besides, I can't stop writing. This story is coming along and I'm kind of feeling it."

"Are you going to let me read it?"

"Of course I will. But not until I'm finished. You never told me when the deadline was. How much time do I have to complete this?"

"At least thirty days. I haven't received the threatening letter from my publisher yet, but my agent said I had thirty days. That was, well, a while ago."

Stephen closed the notebook and placed it on a table in front of him. He looked at me and asked if something was wrong.

"Nope. I spoke to a counselor today. Dr. Manning referred me to one who was very helpful. I'm going to see her three times a week and I hope this is the right move for me. I haven't had one drink all day. Don't really want one, but I just want to be sure my drinking is nothing serious. Aren't you proud of me?"

"Yes, I am. Do what you must and if you need my assistance with anything, let me know. I'm going to try and finish that story soon, but we'll see. I have a lot on my plate, and I'm back on the campaign trail tomorrow. This time I'm going to Ohio."

I rubbed his waves and then touched his thick, sexy lips. "Be careful out there, okay? You know I'm going to worry about you and I'm surprised you haven't taken a break. I saw you and Shawn back in Alabama earlier. All I can do is hope and pray everything will be okay."

"It will be, Raynetta. I can promise you that."

I leaned in to kiss him, but he made it clear he was in no mood for sex. Said he was too tired and he had to get up early for several meetings.

"Tomorrow," he said. "I'll let you have your fun with me tomorrow, but don't expect much from me. My arm is still sore, so I won't be able to throw those pretty legs of yours over my shoulders. I will, however, be able to do other things to excite you. Just wait and see."

"I'm already excited just thinking about it."

"Good. Now other than checking back in with the counselor tomorrow, what's on your agenda?"

"I don't have to meet with the counselor again until the day after tomorrow. But tomorrow Emme and I are going to Florida to help with the clean-up efforts after the storm. That storm caused major damage. Many people lost their homes."

"I know. I heard all about it and I plan to visit early next week. I'm glad you're going there tomorrow. They asked me to stay away because they didn't want people to make a big fuss about me coming."

"I understand. Everybody makes a big fuss over you. After all, you are the president."

I winked and smiled. We returned to the bedroom, and even though Stephen held me that night, the following night he didn't show up. The night after that I didn't even know where he was. I searched the White House with my gown on and couldn't find him anywhere. On the second floor, I'd checked Center Hall, the Dining Room, all guest rooms, and even the Lincoln Bedroom where there had been ghost sightings before. On the third level I checked the Promenade area, the Sunroom and the Penthouse. I even looked in the kitchen, but Stephen wasn't there. When I called his cellphone, he didn't answer. I called Andrew and he wouldn't even tell me where Stephen was at.

"I do know where he's at, but I can't say. I'm sorry, Raynetta."

"I'm his wife, Andrew. I need to know these things and you need to tell me his location right now."

"I can't. He'll contact you soon. And if you're worried about him, I assure you he's fine."

I hung up on him and started to get nervous. So nervous that I met with Chris early the next morning.

"I think he knows something," I said, pacing the floor. "We haven't had sex in two weeks and he keeps making excuses. I caught him staring at me the other day too. I was in my office, and when I looked up, he was in the doorway and hadn't said one word."

"Maybe he was just admiring you like I do. I think you're making too much of this, Raynetta. He did tell you his penis was sore and I'm sure his arm is still bothering him too."

"That could be it, but I'm so worried. I want this over with. I took another home pregnancy test this morning. Negative, negative, negative."

"One day soon it's going to be positive, positive, positive. Just hang on, baby, please hang in there a little while longer."

I wasn't sure if time was on my side, and day-by-day, my gut was sending off bad signals. Stephen never did share with me where he had gone that night, and during a quiet, private dinner he had arranged for the two of us, he finally provided somewhat of an explanation.

"I was probably somewhere writing, Raynetta. I can't stop and I think I'm addicted. Sometimes, I go outside to write and I rarely ever stay in the Oval Office because people always disturb me while I'm in there."

"But I looked all over for you. I called Andrew too and he wouldn't tell me."

"He was ordered not to say a word to anyone. He's just following the rules, but why are you so paranoid? Is there something else troubling you?"

He sipped from his wineglass while gazing at me from across the table. His calm, yet sinister look made me made me squirm in my chair. I swallowed the lump in my throat and reached for the wineglass with apple juice in it to clear my throat.

"No, I'm not paranoid about anything. I just wanted to know where you were. Honestly, I thought you were out somewhere with another woman."

Stephen displayed a smirk on his face. "No, I haven't been interested in any other woman since losing Michelle. That's with the exception of you. I'm very interested in you and I hope we're blessed enough to have a baby soon."

This whole conversation had me feeling some kind of way. The palms of my hands were sweating and I had barely touched the food that had been prepared for me.

"I hope so too, Stephen, but you've kind of backed away from having sex. Is there a reason why?"

He shrugged and wiped across his mouth with a napkin. "We'll get back into the swing of things soon. For now, though, let's dance. I haven't danced with you in a while, and I'm in a mood to hold you in my arms and reminisce about our lives together."

My heart thumped hard against my chest. This didn't feel right, but I tried my best not to let Stephen know my worries. As soft jazz music played in the background, he held me close to him and pressed his cheek against mine. I inhaled his masculine cologne and closed my eyes to take in a moment I couldn't even explain.

"Why are you so nervous?" Stephen whispered. "Your body is trembling and your hands are wet. Does being this close to me make you nervous, Raynetta? I wouldn't think so, but maybe, huh?"

I opened my eyes and backed my head up so I could look at him. "I'm not nervous. I just have a lot of things on my mind."

He didn't inquire. Just held me close and continued to dance with me. Afterwards, we went to the Master Suite. And as soon as I opened the door, a big ass German Shepard with a black shiny coat growled and barked at me. I damn near peed on myself and had jumped in Stephen's arms so I wouldn't get bit.

"Hush Bruce," Stephen ordered. "Go sit down and stop all that barking."

Bruce trotted over to a corner and sat down. I looked at Stephen in awe as he slowly put me down.

"When did you get him? And why is he in this room?"

"I got him last week. He's gotten so attached to me and we've been getting along real good. I've been told that every president should have a dog. They're man's best friend and are very protective of us."

"Well, he shouldn't be in this room. He scares me. Look at how he's looking at me."

Bruce's tongue was hanging out of his mouth and his sharp teeth were on full display.

"He's not going to bother you, Raynetta. And trust me when I say you're going to like him too. It may take some time for you to get used to him, but you will. The trainers said he likes to be around me. That's why he's in here. I want him to feel at home."

I rolled my eyes and hurried into my closet to change. Bruce watched my every move. Stephen kept patting him, and right after we got in bed, Bruce jumped on the bed and lay right in between us.

"This isn't going to work," I said, tossing the covers aside. "I'll go to the Queen's Bedroom to sleep. Bruce can have my spot, but you really need to find another place for him tomorrow."

"I will, but you don't have to leave the bedroom. Relax. I told you he's not going to hurt you."

I wasn't taking any chances, so I left the Master Suite and moseyed into the Queen's Bedroom. I didn't get much sleep, simply because I could sense the clock ticking. Time was running out.

Days later, I started experiencing a heavy discharge. I realized something wasn't right. Then again, it could've been good news. Discharging was one of the symptoms of being pregnant. The pregnancy test I'd taken showed negative again, so I went back to Chris' office to see if he could run more tests. He was out of town for one week, so another female doctor I'd seen in his absence before took care of me. She took all day with my results, and when she finally came into the room, there was a puzzled look on her face. While sitting on the examination table, I immediately started biting my nails.

"Raynetta, before I, uh, discuss your results with you, may I ask you a personal question?"

I shrugged, thinking it had something to do with my book. "Su . . . Sure. Maybe I'll answer, maybe I won't."

"Okay, but how are you and the president? Are the two of you *really* okay?"

"We're fine. Couldn't be better. Why do you ask?"

"Because I read your book and I know how the president is. I don't want to cause any additional problems for the two of you, but you have a sexually transmitted disease. Have you ever had Chlamydia before?"

My eyes were about to break from their sockets. My heartrate increased and the punch to my gut made me grab my stomach.

"What did you say? Are you serious? No, there must be some kind of mistake. This is a joke, isn't it? I don't have anything called Chlamydia."

"I'm afraid you do. I think you need to have a serious conversation with the president. Maybe he can shed some light on this situation for you. Meanwhile, I want to let you know that your medical history is very confidential. This stays between me, you and the president, okay?"

I was speechless. Quite embarrassed too. No wonder Stephen had spoken about his penis hurting so much—he knew damn well why. The only reason he didn't want to have sex with me was because of this. I didn't have to think long and hard about who might have given him this disease. Photos of him and Florence Green had been plastered all over the news. He had been dishonest; I would put any amount of money on it that sex between him and that sleazy whore led to this. That was exactly where he was the other night. I couldn't get back to the White House fast enough. And as Secret Service drove me back there, I started searching for information about Florence Green on my cellphone. The most noticeable thing was a sex tape of her. I started to watch and all I could do was cover my mouth. She was nasty. They were nasty. Stephen was nasty and how in the hell could he let this happen?

By the time I reached the White House, I was livid. Secret Service opened the door for me, and I rushed out of the SUV to go inside.

"Raynetta," the agent yelled. "You forgot your purse. Is everything okay?"

I snatched my purse from him and tucked it underneath my arm. "Hell no everything is not okay. But it will be soon."

I stormed inside, looking for Stephen. He was in the Oval Office with his head down, writing something in a notebook. As soon as he saw me he lifted his head.

"Baby, I'm telling you this story I'm writing is getting real good," he boasted. "I can't wait for you to check it out."

"Before I check it out, why don't you check this out and tell me all about it."

I hit the play button and slammed my cellphone on his desk. The video of Florence Green started to play. We both could hear the slurping, moaning and groaning and see naked bodies. Stephen glanced at my cellphone and shrugged.

"Okay. Where are you going with this? Do you want to polish me off like that too?"

"I already have and I totally regret putting my mouth on that *thing*, especially when you've been screwing around with that nasty chick."

"In my opinion, she's skilled not nasty. But why are you accusing me of being with her? I already told you about the photo her ex-boyfriend took. Nothing happened and she will tell you that too. Would you like to stoop low and call her?"

"I'm sure you have her number on speed dial. I thought we were totally done with this, but yet again, here we are."

Stephen stood and closed the notebook on his desk. "Something is severely wrong with you, Raynetta. You love drama and I don't know if you are capable of conducting yourself like grown folks. I'm not going to keep entertaining your foolishness and if I have been intimate with someone, you'd be the first to know. I said I haven't, so if you don't have anything else to discuss, please leave and go do something to keep yourself busy."

"I did do something else to keep myself busy. I went to the doctor today and you know what she told me, Stephen? You probably want to sit down or get your gun ready for that whore you've been with. That way, you can blow her damn brains out for giving you a STD and passing it on to me."

His face twisted. He cocked his head back and sighed. "Get out of here with that mess. You have lost your damn mind. Either that or the alcohol got you tripping. More so slipping."

I was at a loss for words. It hadn't even crossed my mind that I could've gotten this from Chris. He was a doctor—if anyone practiced safe sex he would. Then again, what if Stephen wasn't lying? I surely didn't know who to turn to, but I had to back off of this until I spoke to Chris. I couldn't stop thinking if I was the one who had given Stephen a STD. If I had, he would've said something by now. Either way, my tone decreased.

"I haven't been drinking, but I was just trying to see if you were lying about being involved with Florence. I'll let you get back to what you were doing. Forgive me for the intrusion."

I turned to walk away, but hearing Stephen's voice caused me to halt my steps.

"Maybe you should go back to the doctor to make sure you're okay. Dr. Manning should be able to clear up everything for you. After all, he's been your doctor for a long time, hasn't he?"

My heart eased past my stomach and hit the floor. My face had been cracked too, but I pivoted and pretended like his comment didn't shock me.

"Dr. Manning is out of town. I'll be sure to follow up with him soon."

"You should follow up with him, because he was definitely the one who gave you a STD, not me. Feel free to come have a seat so we can discuss this little matter. After we're done, maybe you'll be able to tell me what you think I should do about this."

My body trembled. While I wanted to leave, I needed to stay and hear how much he knew. I didn't think he would harm me in the Oval Office—that I was sure of.

I walked over to the sofa and slowly sat down. Calm as ever, Stephen came from behind his desk and sat on the same sofa as me. He rubbed his hands together and started to tell me how much he knew.

"First let me say that even after all we've endured, I still thought we would one day be able to move on and patch up things. I was looking forward to you having our child and I was hyped about all the sex between us. But then, Raynetta, I started having some issues with my dick. I didn't know what was wrong, until I had my doctor check things out for me. He confirmed my little problem, and I started thinking how something like this could happen. I hadn't been with anyone since Michelle, so the only other person who could've put me in this position was you. It didn't take long for me to figure out the other man in your life was Dr. Manning. I sensed something while we were in his office that day, and that's why I didn't say much. It was how you looked at him and he looked at you. The way he touched you and you smiled. How he disrespected me, yet you said not one word. I was going to kill you the other night, but you surprised me with your gun. That was another thing I wasn't aware of, but I decided to put things off and wait for another day. The sad thing about all of this is I believe Dr. Manning took advantage of you. He told you he loved you and tricked you into doing some things you probably didn't always agree with. I don't even think you love him, but in your mind, any man out there is better than me."

I fumbled with my hands and started to talk my way out of this. A slow tear fell down my face; I wiped it.

"I've only loved one man in my life and that continues to be you. I was hurt, Stephen, and I didn't know where else to turn. I had high hopes for us too, but I just couldn't find it in my heart to forgive you. Chris was there for me, and before I knew it, he started talking about how we could be together, have a peaceful life and about a baby."

Stephen nodded. "Yep, a baby. My baby who you were planning on raising with him and finally getting your happily ever after. I get how badly you wanted it, but come on, Raynetta. Did you really think you could have it with him? That fool is sleeping with several of his patients and he's even involved with the counselor he recommended to you. I guess you were too blind to see what was really going on, mainly because any man would do. How sad and unfortunate is that?"

Stephen got up to pour himself a drink. He was too calm for me and you'd better believe it made me extremely nervous.

"Would you like something to drink?" he asked.

"No, but I would like to say I'm sorry for all of this. I guess we'll never understand each other's motives, but I really wish you would see things from my point of view."

"Trust me, Raynetta, I have. I have beaten myself up when I think about all that I've done, but sweetheart, your bullshit supersedes mine and then some. At some point, I had to realize you're not cut out for this. And unfortunately, my mother was right. The first lady position is too much for you to handle. Therefore, it's time for me to free you."

Whenever he used words like that, it was time for me to go. I had no kind of weapon on me to protect myself, so I stood and took another deep breath.

"I'll go and wash my hands to all of this. You can tell the American people whatever you wish and maybe down the road the two of us will be able to see eye-to-eye on certain things."

He didn't respond. Just tossed back the alcohol while gazing at me. I was so tense and could feel sweat building on my forehead. My skin was getting sticky and my coochie was still in need of medical attention.

"Pack as much as you can tonight," Stephen said. "I'll have the rest sent to you. Secret Service will take you to where you need to go or you can take Marine One to another city. That's what I highly recommend because, due to my temper, I prefer not to be anywhere near you."

I didn't argue with him about that. The further away from him the better. I rushed upstairs to the Executive Residence and hurried to gather some of my things so I could go. I was undeniably afraid Stephen was going to do something to me, but I held onto his words about us living far away from each other. That was a good sign he was willing to wash his hands to this too. I threw much of what I needed in the suitcase, and took about two minutes to close it because it was so full. I even tucked my gun in my purse, just in case I had to use it. The second I left the Master Suite, the agent who had been taking me everywhere I needed to go was right there.

"Are you ready?" he asked. "Where would you like for me to take you?"

"To Marine One. Take me to New York, LaGuardia Airport, please. I'll be fine after that and I don't need you to follow me."

"I'll have to make sure that's approved by the president. As far as I know, it's still my job to protect you."

"No, the president knows I'm leaving by myself. You can confirm it with him if you want."

"I will, but allow me to carry your suitcase. I'll get you cleared for take-off on Marine One and get you to New York as soon as possible."

I thanked the agent and walked beside him as we made our way outside and across the South Lawn to Marine One. A bit paranoid, I kept turning around and lifting my dark shades to see if Stephen or that damn dog were somewhere lurking. I didn't see them, but a handful of reporters from the media were there. I had to wait a few minutes for things to get situated with Marine One. Several reporters inquired about where I was going.

"On vacation," I replied. "I'll be back in a week, maybe two."

"Are you going on vacation without the president?"

I nodded and looked around for him again. "Yes, but he may join me later. Have a good one and see you all when I get back."

I wasn't sure how Stephen was going to break the news to everyone, but I didn't want to say anything stupid that would make me look bad.

"Your suitcase is on Marine One," the agent said. "And the pilot is ready to go."

The propellers started to circle and the breeze picked up. I hurried up the steps and tripped because I was moving so fast. I snapped my head to look behind me again—no Stephen. Right after I got on the helicopter, I checked all of the seats to make sure I was alone. I even looked in the bathroom; it was all clear. The pilot stood near the doorway, shaking the agent's hand.

"To LaGuardia Airport, correct?" the pilot said.

"Yes. Please take her there and contact the White House to confirm the first lady's arrival."

The pilot nodded and looked at me. "It shouldn't be a long ride to New York. Can I get you anything before we take off?"

"No," I said. "I'm just ready to go, if you don't mind."

My stomach was in a knot—my nerves rattled with each passing minute. I was anxious to leave and I kept looking outside to see if Stephen was anywhere in sight.

The Secret Service agent exited the helicopter and minutes later the door was shut. The pilot confirmed "ready for takeoff" over the intercom and within a few more minutes the helicopter was off the ground. My stomach still felt queasy and my throat ached badly. I was ready to go live a new quiet life, and if Stephen and I ever had a chance to revisit all of this one day, maybe, the door would be open. I had some regrets, particularly with Dr. Manning. When it came to him, it was a wrap. He would never hear from me again—I couldn't stop thinking about that dirty bastard. I wasn't sure if Stephen would do anything to him or not. At this point, the only person I was concerned about was me.

Marine One was up in the air, but it seemed like it kept flying in circles. When I looked out the tinted window, I could see that the pilot kept circling the White House. I hadn't a clue why he was flying in circles, but when I squinted, I could see Stephen standing on the Truman Balcony, looking even sexier than the day I'd met him. He stood near the edge and the helicopter was so close that the wind stirring from the propellers blew his suit jacket open. His suspenders showed and with several buttons on his shirt undone, I could see part of his chest. One hand was in his pocket and his other hand gripped a glass. That stupid dog was next to him barking. The helicopter was now in the same spot and hadn't moved. Stephen could definitely see me; I could see him. He winked and lifted his glass in the air. Right as he pivoted to go back inside, Marine One started moving again. Tears welled in my eyes and my whole body felt like someone was poking me with knifes. My thoughts were all over the place, but when I heard the pilot's voice, I snapped out of it.

"This is as far as I go," he said over the intercom.

I wasn't sure what he'd meant by that, until I heard the swooshing sound of the loud wind. My head snapped to the side and I saw a parachute floating in the air. I hurried to remove my seatbelt, but as soon as I stood, I smashed my hands over my ears to protect them from a thunderous sound that got louder and sounded like an explosion. Fire quickly spread and thick smoke clogged my throat. After that, I couldn't remember a thing.

Dr. Christopher Manning

I was in Miami for a family medicine conference. It only lasted for six hours, and after it was over I was free to enjoy the rest of my trip. It felt good to get away from the office and relax. I didn't have to deal with my griping patients who sometimes got on my nerves. That was with the exception of Raynetta. She had issues, but her issues could be immediately resolved. All she had to do was leave that ignorant fool in the White House and her problems would be solved. To say I hated Stephen *Coward* Jefferson would be an understatement. From the time he'd gotten elected, I despised everything about him. He was an embarrassment to successful black men, like me, who needed to be role models for so many children in America. Every time I saw him on TV, I turned it off because I couldn't stand to look at him. He was too damn arrogant and I didn't approve of the reckless policies he had put in place. As a life-long Republican, I couldn't get on board with the direction he was attempting to take this country. All he cared about was trying to save niggas who didn't need to be saved. Street thugs who blamed cops for their problems, while they were out there killing each other every day. None of it made sense, and to have a president who catered to those thugs was sickening. He did nothing for people who pulled themselves up by the bootstraps and worked hard for everything they'd had. That was me. I made no excuses for growing up poor. I went to school, got an education and became a doctor. Nothing was given to me. Not one single thing, so for black people to sit around complaining all the time about how immoral this country was, those people were a joke. I firmly believed they needed to seek another country to live in because America provided plenty of opportunities. We were free to do whatever our hearts desired and there was nothing that prevented black folks from reaching their highest potential. What prohibited progress was people being lazy. I got sick of hearing the excuses from them and from the president. His socialist policies were why so many blacks loved him. For the next couple of years, they could expect more handouts, and all slavery reparations would do was make them even lazier. I was so disgusted, and if Raynetta or I couldn't put an end to this madness soon, I planned to make preparations to run for president. Mr. Jefferson needed a serious contender. With so many Republicans feeling the same way as I did, I could very well find myself in the Oval Office someday, putting forth every effort to make this country great once again. Until then, the best woman I could have by my side was Raynetta. I had always felt something solid with her, and the first time I made love to her was special. She was so distraught about Stephen being with another woman; all I could do was comfort her, each time she'd told me about his affair with Michelle. As she provided more dirt about the president, I wanted to help her find a way out. I also wanted to do whatever I could to get him out of office. If it meant causing him harm, fine. If it meant running against him in a few years and beating the pants off him, I was prepared to do that too. No matter what, he had to go.

I had just gotten out of the shower and was in my hotel suite getting dressed for a dinner date tonight. After my divorce, I'd started dating again. My previous wife was a black woman with too much attitude. All she'd done was spend my money as fast as I made it and she tried to order me around. She wanted to be the boss, but without me, she didn't have a pot to piss in or a window to throw it out of. I was so glad to be rid of her. I didn't approve of what I'd had to pay her in spousal support, but her attorney convinced the female judge that I was the one at fault for causing our marriage to end. I was blamed for cheating, being physically and mentally abusive to her, and she claimed I had abandoned our son. My occupation prevented me from being at home all the time, and as for cheating on her, yes, I had. I got sick of her bitching all the time, and to me, she was just another gold-digging, lazy woman who wanted to sit at home while I did all the work. I never wanted to involve myself with another woman like her again; therefore, I chose to date only white women going forward. Raynetta, however, was the exception.

As I sat on the bed, putting on my Salvatore Ferragamo loafers, my cellphone vibrated. I reached for it on the nightstand and held it close to my ear.

"Dr. Manning," I said then slapped my face with aftershave. I couldn't make out who the person on the other end of the phone was because she was crying. "Hello. Who is this?"

"Chris, this is Nancy. I'm so upset with you. How could you do this?"

I sighed and stood to tuck my silk shirt into my slacks. Nancy was always upset about something, but I didn't have time to deal with her issues tonight. She'd made it clear that she wanted to marry me, but in no way did I see her in my future.

"How could I do what?" I asked, as if I really cared. "What did I do to upset you this time, Nancy?"

"I just saw my doctor. She told me I have Chlamydiaaaaa!" she cried. "If you've been faithful to me, how in the hell did I get this!"

I couldn't believe she was calling me with this nonsense. I didn't bother to respond. Just hung up on her and turned my phone off when she called again. How dare she call me to say something stupid like that? I never admitted to being faithful to her, and I damn sure didn't give her Chlamydia. She must've been drinking again; this time she'd gone too far. I sat on the bed again and lightly touched my goatee. Drunk or not, I didn't think she would lie about something pertaining to a STD. As far as I knew, she hadn't been seeing anyone else, other than me. My thoughts quickly turned to Raynetta. What if she contracted a STD from the president? With all the women he'd been with it damn sure was possible. I hurried to pick up the phone to call her. Her voicemail came on.

"Hey Sweetheart. Give me a call when you can. I need to speak to you about something. I miss you and I should be home in a few days. Can't wait to see you."

I hung up and started pondering again about what Nancy had implied. My mind traveled back to several weeks ago when I'd gone to Vegas and had sex with a prostitute. There were times when I opted to go there to satisfy my sexual cravings and fetishes. I always protected myself, but the sex was so intense that the condom ripped. I wondered if I had contracted anything from her—this was messed up if I had. In no way could I explain something like this to Raynetta, and the more I'd thought about it, I started to panic and pace the floor. What if I gave a STD to her? I couldn't stop thinking about the consequences, and after calling her three more times, she still hadn't answered.

"Baby, it's me again. Listen, I really need you to call me back. As soon as you get this message, call me. Please."

I was so disturbed by this that I made a logical decision not to go on my date. I waited for Raynetta to call back, but by midnight I still hadn't heard from her. Maybe she was mad at me about this. Had I screwed up? It surely seemed like it and I was so furious with myself for hooking up with a prostitute. Damn! My fist pounded the bed and I started to pace the floor again. I wouldn't be able to calm down until I heard from Raynetta. I needed to hear from her soon, but when I turned on the TV and saw what had occurred earlier today, I covered my mouth in shock. I used the remote to click from one news channel to another, just to be sure what was being reported was true. There was an explosion on Marine One. The first lady, my sweet Raynetta, had been killed. I couldn't believe it. I didn't want to believe it and there was no way in hell this was happening. Panicking even more, I had to get out of there and go back to Washington. Raynetta feared that something tragic would happen to her; she mentioned the president knew something. If he knew about us, it was right up his alley to do something like this. He was responsible for this and I needed to let it be known to the FBI right away.

I hurried to pack and leave. But right when I opened the door, I came face-to-face with a heavyset white man who blocked me from exiting.

"Are you Dr. Christopher Manning?" he asked.

"Yes, I am. Who wants to know?"

He replied by raising his fist and punching me in my face. The punch sent me stumbling backwards before I hit the floor. I couldn't even defend myself. His blows were too powerful, and after numerous punches to my bloody face, he gripped my head with his strong hands.

"Before you go," he said, ready to snap my neck. "The president wants to thank you for everything you've done."

I wasn't even allowed a second to tell him to go to hell.

President of the United States, Stephen C. Jefferson

After six long months, many Americans were still mourning the first lady's death. In public, my devastation showed and I don't think it was one person in the country who didn't feel sorry for me. Well, some didn't, but the majority did. I had received many cards, letters, flowers and condolences. Many reporters had cried with me and they all believed the bomb on Marine One was put there to assassinate me. Unfortunately, Raynetta just happened to be on it. She was on her way to a vacation spot where I was supposed to meet her later. That was the spin and there was really no other way to look at it. With the election of my second term coming up in the next two years, it was pretty much set in stone. I had overcome a lot, and I was viewed as a president who showed much strength. I didn't want to take all the credit, especially since, for the good of the nation, the White House staff worked together. Secret Service kept many secrets for presidents and they would never tell a soul what actually happened at 1600 Pennsylvania Avenue. That was why many presidents had gotten away with so much bullshit, including murder. I wasn't the first; I damn sure wouldn't be the last. Nonetheless, I had to face questions from the FBI who didn't have to subpoena me because I was willing to talk with or without a lawyer.

"Do you know anyone who would've wanted to kill Dr. Christopher Manning? His body was found stuffed in his trunk and we know the first lady was one of his patients."

"I'd only met the doctor once. He seemed like a nice man and Raynetta spoke highly of him."

The FBI Director nodded and stared at me as if he was looking through me. It was his job to sense when someone was lying; I could tell he was thoroughly examining me.

"What about your mother? Have you heard from her yet? She just vanished into thin air. A warrant has been issued for her arrest for missing her court dates. Do you have any idea where we can find her?"

"I'm well aware of the warrant. My mother never should've been released from jail and I knew she would flee. There's no telling what country she's in by now, but if she ever contacts me, I'll be sure to let someone know."

"I won't keep you much longer, Mr. President, but I do have a few more questions for you. Did you ever make any attempts to harm the first lady? And how did you feel about Mr. McNeil being related to her? Were you angry about it and did you ever threaten him? We still haven't found the person responsible for his death. His family wants answers."

I shrugged again and looked at Andrew who stood next to me in silence.

"Hell, there are plenty of families who want and deserve answers. All those black men and women being killed by dirty, racist cops, their families want answers too. There is no question that Mr. McNeil and I didn't like each other, but he had a lot of enemies. I hope you've checked your long list of suspects and checked them twice. I'm sure the killer is somewhere on there."

"I know he is, but what about the first lady? You didn't answer. Did you ever make any attempts to cause her harm?"

"We had our problems, but she was the love of my life. I never did or said anything to intentionally cause her harm."

"I thought Michelle Peoples was the love of your life?"

"She was too. A man is allowed to have two loves, maybe more, isn't he?"

The FBI Director smirked. "I guess he is. Thanks for your time, and if I have any additional questions, I'll be back."

"You're always welcome."

He smiled and left. Andrew sighed and looked at me as I sat calmly at my desk.

"That was not good," Andrew said. "Are you worried? You know there are certain things that I know, I'm not supposed to know, but I do know."

"Of course you know everything, but I trust you, Andrew. I've done so for a very long time, and if I didn't, you would've disappeared too."

We shook hands, and for the record, I wasn't concerned with the FBI. While there were plenty of good men and women who worked for the agency, the FBI had issues too. And as a black president, I knew how deep those issues were. The last thing they wanted to do was fuck with me. The director knew it would be a big . . . huge mistake.

Several weeks later, we all sat in the Oval Office waiting for the midterm results. Things were looking good and the Republicans were on the verge of losing control of both the House and Senate. There were numerous Independents on the ballots in each state too, but they were pretty much on board with doing exactly what I needed them to do.

"Yes!" Sam shouted as another Republican incumbent had lost. Motherfucker had been in Congress for nearly twenty years and hadn't done one positive thing. It was good to see the American people had finally had enough.

We high-fived each other and waited patiently for more votes to come in. By nine o'clock that night, it was a complete bloodbath. There were less than thirty Republicans still trying to hold on in the House and Senate. Barely enough to keep their seats warm, because that's all they could do pertaining to legislation. None of their votes would matter and I was thrilled about getting every single item on my agenda passed.

"This is beautiful," Andrew said while on his knees with his hands clenched together. "I . . . I can't believe this, Mr. President. While I knew the Republicans would lose plenty of seats, I never, ever could have imagined this. Thank you for hanging in there. Thank you so much for not giving up. I know you've been through a lot, but this is your moment, Sir. The time is now."

I couldn't have agreed with him more. The time was now and the American people had showed up and showed out. Not even Russia could fuck with our democracy—not as long as I was president. The victory party had started, and right after Shawn and numerous other newly elected Senators called to thank me for my efforts in helping them get elected, I joined numerous guests in the East Room. We partied hard; many people couldn't stop talking about me losing Raynetta and being single.

"I'll find my queen one of these days," I said to a group of women from my administration. "She's out there and I'm sure she'll make me a better man."

"I have a niece who adores you, Mr. President," Pat said. "She's beautiful, educated and single. Can I set the two of you up on a date?"

I laughed. "Not yet. I'm still working through some things after losing the first lady. When I'm ready I'll let you know."

"Pat, your niece may have to stand in a long line," said Gabrielle. "And even though we know your heart is still broken, Mr. President, please learn to live a little. Don't you go crazy up in this White House without a good woman by your side. I hope you do find someone else who'll make you just as happy as the first lady did. I know she's looking down from heaven and is so proud of you."

"I'm sure she is too."

I excused myself from the women, because Raynetta was not the person I wanted to talk about. It was over and done with—I damn sure didn't want to look back. While I had contributed to the demise of my marriage, I couldn't let Raynetta off the hook. We'd both had tragic upbringings that affected us in every way. But I didn't feel sorry for people who sat around feeling sorry for themselves, who didn't want to admit their fuck-ups and did nothing to help cure their problems. Life-long problems that caused Raynetta to blame me for everything and concoct sneaky plans to harm me. I tried to change the outcome, but her manipulation became unbearable. She turned out to be exactly like my mother—what a damn shame that was.

After the party was over and nearly everyone had left for the night, I returned to the Oval Office. I sat behind the Resolute desk, relaxed as ever and thinking hard. Referring to the Obamas, there was no black president and his queen in the White House this time, but this was my story and I owned it. Unlike any other president who came before me, I'd had a different way of getting things accomplished. My eight-year term would enable me to claim the top spot in history, and even though my close circle had shrunk tremendously, sometimes, that needed to happen when a person was on the road to greatness. Through my leadership, all Americans would prosper more than they had done in the past one hundred years. Black people would be able to build things, racism would be rejected, cops would be jailed for shooting unarmed Americans, guns laws would change and our nation would be more united than ever. I wanted people to be excited about the future. I still had some flaws, but when all was said and done, I, Stephen C. Jefferson, would get full credit for putting America on the right track. Wasn't that what really mattered or would some Americans continue to believe my personal life mattered more than the policies I'd put in place as president? In order to be classified as a decent president, was it necessary for me to keep a first lady like Raynetta by my side and continue the behind-closed-doors dysfunction? In my opinion it wasn't, and in due time I intended to find a partner I could trust and who made me feel like Michelle had. Until then, I had no worries, other than the FBI snooping around. I felt the heat, but the heat hadn't turned to fire yet.

My eyelids fluttered and her soft voice snapped me out of my thoughts. I couldn't concentrate on what she was doing to me, because my mind was focused more on the entire successful evening.

"Mr. President, are you into this or not?" she said then wiped across her sexy, wet lips. "If not, I can go back to Virginia and come back another time."

"There is no other time better than now."

I closed my eyes, and as she resumed, I wiggled my tie away from my neck. Unbuttoned my shirt and let her have her way with me that night. I wasn't a perfect president and I said I had flaws, didn't I? According to the presidential playbook, every last one of us did. The world just didn't know the truth about the most powerful men in the world. At least, I was willing to tell all of it, well, some of it in a book.

CPSIA information can be obtained
at www.ICGtesting.com
Printed in the USA
LVHW090644291019
635575LV00006BA/1032/P

9 781986 821186